Taking a deep breath, she opened her eyes and found Gavin staring at her.

He crooked a finger at her and then pointed toward the hallway. She followed him outside the door of Sam's bedroom.

"That's a first," Gavin said. "In six months. Sam has been coming into my bedroom and staring at me, making sure I'm not going to leave him forever. The way, in his eyes, his mother did."

Her heart twisted at his words. "He's had a hard time. You've all had a hard time."

Gavin gave a slow nod, and she was all too aware of his height, his power, his masculinity. "Yeah, we have. Who would have known a sound machine would make such a difference?"

She shrugged, knowing that a sound machine was the secret to a night of sleep for her. "Yeah. Who would have known?"

"Thank you," he said, and lowered his head toward hers.

She caught her breath.

He squeezed her arm. "Get some sleep."

Sara nearly collapsed in a combination of relief and strange disappointment. She stared after him and felt a flip in her stomach. Yes, she definitely needed more sleep.

* * *

ROYAL BABIES:
A new generation of little princes—and princesses!

Dear Reader,

We're back in Chantaine with a new family. The royal Tarisses have come to town! Times are hard in the small country of Sergenia. The economy is failing and there are threats against the Tarisse royal family. Princesses Sasha and Tabitha are sent to Chantaine to wait out the instability. The princesses are instructed to live as commoners for their safety and to adopt different identities.

Princess Sasha goes from being a celebrated concert pianist representing her country...to Sara Smith, a nanny for the young children of single dad Gavin Sinclair.

Can you imagine trying to make that switch? Have you ever been forced out of your comfort zone?

Gavin and his young children are suffering from a huge loss. Despite the fact that Sara has her own worries, she gets caught up in their lives and grows attached to all of them. This is supposed to be temporary. But as time goes on, she wonders how she can ever go back to the life she led before.

I hope you enjoy meeting this new royal family and also getting a chance to see how the royal Devereaux family is doing.

I would love to hear from you at leannebanks1@gmail.com. My website is leannebanks.com, and I can also be found on Facebook.

Wishing you the best in life and love!

Leanne Banks

A Princess Under the Mistletoe

Leanne Banks

Recycling programs for this product may not exist in your area.

ISBN-13: 978-0-373-65928-9

A Princess Under the Mistletoe

This edition published by arrangement with Harlequin Books S.A.

For questions and comments about the quality of this book, please contact us at CustomerService@Harlequin.com.

Printed in U.S.A.

Leanne Banks is a *New York Times* bestselling author with over sixty books to her credit. A book lover and romance fan from even before she learned to read, Leanne has always treasured the way that books allow us to go to new places and experience the lives of wonderful characters. Always ready for a trip to the beach, Leanne lives in Virginia with her family and her Pomeranian muse.

Books by Leanne Banks

Harlequin Special Edition

Royal Babies

A Royal Christmas Proposal
How to Catch a Prince
A Home for Nobody's Princess
The Princess and the Outlaw

The Doctor Takes a Princess
The Prince's Texas Bride
Royal Holiday Baby

Montana Mavericks: 20 Years in the Saddle!

Maverick for Hire

The Fortunes of Texas: Welcome to Horseback Hollow

Happy New Year, Baby Fortune!

Montana Mavericks: Rust Creek Cowboys

The Maverick & The Manhattanite

Montana Mavericks: Back in the Saddle

A Maverick for the Holidays

Montana Mavericks: The Texans are Coming!

A Maverick for Christmas

Visit the Author Profile page at Harlequin.com for more titles.

This book is dedicated to all the single parents
and all the people who step in to help
when things get crazy. You are everyday heroes!

Prologue

"Your Highness, Princess Fredericka Devereaux, please allow me to introduce you to Princesses Sasha and Tabitha Tarisse," Paul Hamburg said as the beautiful princess who had arranged for Sasha and her sister's safety swept into the room.

Sasha stood and dragged her younger sister to her feet. The past few months had been nonstop terror for her and the rest of her family, the royal Tarisses of Sergenia. Her country had suffered a terrible economic downturn during the past three years, and the citizens had grown angry and impatient. Just lately they'd turned their anger and frustration against the royal family. There'd been threats. Sasha had barely escaped a beating and her sister Tabitha had nearly been kidnapped.

As much as Sasha had despised the idea of leaving her country, her brother, Alexander, had convinced her that all of them must leave, at least temporarily. One of the royal advisors had negotiated with Princess Fredericka for the Tarisse siblings to come to Chantaine, a peaceful Mediterranean island country.

"Please call me Ericka," she said, moving toward the two women. "You must be tired. Would you like some tea?" she asked.

"Yes, please," Sasha said, hoping she'd made the right choice about coming to Chantaine. She and her sister had left everything familiar to them back in Sergenia. What if this move was a disaster? Despite Princess Ericka's cool, blond beauty, the woman's eyes held a world of compassion.

Ericka nodded toward the assistant. "Please get some tea and pastries."

Sasha patted the loose chignon at the back of her neck. "We're grateful you've welcomed us to your country," Sasha said. "You'll forgive us if we're not at our most congenial."

"Because we've been tricked," Tabitha added with a scowl. "We made an agreement with our brother, Alex. He told us he would meet us in Chantaine, but he has disappeared."

"Oh, I'm so sorry. Do you have any idea where he could be?" Ericka asked.

Tabitha crossed her arms over her chest, her eyes nearly spitting sparks. "Who knows? He may be roaming the mountains on the border of our country. Or he may be partying in Italy."

"Tabitha," Sasha said in an admonishing voice. "I apologize," she said to Ericka.

"I can understand some of your frustrations. I've dealt with my share of sibling skirmishes."

The assistant returned with tea and snacks and the

three women sat down. Although Sasha was hungry, she couldn't imagine being able to swallow a bite. She did well to sip the tea.

"It's my pleasure to welcome you to Chantaine," Princess Ericka said. "But as you know, we have several conditions for your visit here. These are for both your safety and the safety of our citizens. I'm sure you've been told you'll need to assume different identities. You're not to reveal your true identity to anyone. Sasha, I know you're a talented concert pianist, but while you are here, we ask that you not play in public."

Sasha nodded, fighting a stab of sadness. Music had always provided her with peace. Even though she'd known that giving up her concert career would be part of the bargain, she couldn't help the emptiness she felt.

"You can, however, play in private. We'll try to make sure you have access to a piano during your stay."

"Thank you," Sasha said. "It would be difficult for me if I couldn't play at all."

"Tabitha, we're working on finding a position for you within the next few days. In the meantime, the two of you can stay here. However, and this is hard for me to say, you must not appear in public together."

Tabitha's face fell. "Never?"

"This is not forever," Ericka reminded her. "This is just during your stay while your country resolves its current turmoil. It's for your safety. Think about it. If the two of you are seen together, it's more likely that someone will figure out your true identities."

Her heart wrenching at the realization of what would be required of both her sister and herself, Sasha slipped her hand through her sister's. "We will do what we must, but what do we do about our brother, Alex?"

Ericka looked at Paul Hamburg expectantly.

"We'll make inquiries, but we must tread carefully with the princesses staying in Chantaine. We don't want to arouse suspicion," he said.

"But we have contacts who have contacts," Ericka said.

Paul sighed. "Yes, we do."

"Then, although I know that you don't take orders from me, I hope you will give this your best discreet effort."

"I will," he said.

"Thank you," she said before turning back to the sisters. "Now let me tell you about Chantaine."

Despite the grim situation, Princess Ericka regaled Sasha and Tabitha with tales of Chantaine's beauty, temperate climate, numerous beaches and kind citizens. Sasha began to relax a tiny bit, or perhaps she'd been tense for so long that her body couldn't maintain the adrenaline rush any longer.

"This is a delicate subject, but as I said, you will need to use other identities. Have you thought about what names you'd like to use during your stay here?"

Tabitha tossed her long, dark hair. "I was thinking Gypsy Rose," she said.

Sasha rolled her eyes. "We've already discussed this. We need names that won't draw attention."

Tabitha lifted a dark eyebrow and shot her a look of challenge. "All right, Miss Sensible. What have you chosen?"

"Sara," Sasha said. "Sara Smith. I chose a first name with the same letter as my real name, and one that sounds similar, so I'll have a better chance of answering to it. Can you top that for ordinary?"

Tabitha sets her lips in a pout that had been known to make a hundred men race to do her bidding. Sasha could tell that she'd hit on Tabitha's competitive streak by the glint in her sister's eye.

"I don't suppose I could get away with Jane Doe," Tabitha said. "Isn't that what an American would choose?"

Princess Ericka chuckled. "I think not. Let's go with Martin for your last name. It's a common name in Chantaine and Europe."

Tabitha sighed. "Then I suppose I'll have to go with Jane Martin if I'm going to beat Sasha at her game." She cleared her throat. "Oh, I'm sorry. I meant to say Sara."

Chapter One

One year later...

From the porch, Sara heard the sound of screaming. If she hadn't known better, she might have assumed the sound wasn't human. The sound of scrambling footsteps followed and the door opened.

A tall, rumpled-looking man stared at her as he held a screaming red-faced baby, and a young boy seemed to be attached to his leg.

"Are you Sara?" he asked, out of breath. "Sara Smith. The palace sent you?"

"Yes," she said.

He looked her up and down. "Thank you for coming," he said over the cries of the baby in his arms. "No offense, but you look terribly young. Are you old enough to be a nanny?"

Sara had scrubbed her face clean of cosmetics with

the exception of lip gloss. All part of her temporary new role. She certainly didn't need to wear the heavy stage makeup required of a concert pianist. "I'll take that as a compliment," she said. "I'm twenty-seven."

"Oh," he said, surprise crossing his features. "I never would have guessed." The baby let out another howl. "We're having a rough day, so if you want to give them juice and cookies to calm them down, that's fine."

He dragged his foot, with the attached child down the hallway. "This is Sam," he said, nodding toward the boy.

"Hello, Sam," Sara said tentatively. Although she'd known the family she was going to be working with was still reeling from a loss, this wasn't exactly what she'd envisioned.

"And I'm holding Adelaide," the man said. "As you can see, she's a handful."

"Yes," Sara said. "Mr. Sinclair?"

"Oh," he said, shaking his head. "Call me Gavin. You may be calling me some other names as the day wears on," he said with a crooked smile on his face.

She met his gaze for a long moment and saw a combination of weariness and determined humor in his chocolate-brown eyes. He wasn't conventionally handsome. Sara had met much more smoothly handsome men in her life. His rough strong features might have put her off, but his dark eyebrows and hard jaw were offset by that crooked smile and eyes that crinkled with humor even as his daughter shrieked directly into his ear.

He looked at Adelaide and stroked her cheek. "Sweetheart, you're going to be fine." He glanced at Sara. "She's been cranky lately. I don't know what's bothering her. Drooling up a storm, nose running, but no fever. Maybe a midmorning nap will help. Let me show you where everything is," he said. He held out his hand to Sam. "Help me out, bud. Let's show the pretty lady around."

Sam reluctantly detached himself from Gavin's leg and held Gavin's hand with both of his while Gavin explained the layout of the house, which, in addition to the master bedroom, contained a small nursery in the back, a laundry room and two additional small bedrooms, one filled with the little boy's books and toys. The other was positioned between the nursery and what she assumed was Sam's room."This is your bedroom. I hope you don't mind sharing a bathroom with Sam," Gavin said.

"Not at all," she said, appreciating the way the morning sun shone through the window. The room was small and decorated with neutral quality linens, and it felt cozy. The whole house felt safe. A trickle of relief slid through her. This could work, she thought.

Gavin continued down the hall and waved his hand toward another bedroom containing a desk and computer along with exercise equipment. "Here's the master. As you can tell, I've been trying to work some at home, but I haven't been all that successful." Adelaide had quieted and was letting out little moans.

Gavin turned again toward her. "You've seen the small formal parlor. We're using the den as a playroom. Lots of toys and books, movies and favorite television shows. Feel free to use whatever you need."

An old upright piano against the far wall immediately grabbed Sara's attention. She gasped in delight. It was all she could do not to race over and feel the keys beneath her fingers. "You have a piano."

Gavin nodded. "You play?"

In concert halls all over the world, she thought, rubbing her hands together. But not very much lately. She shrugged. "A little."

"I can't promise it's been tuned recently," he warned. "The piano hasn't been a priority."

"Of course," she said, putting her hands behind her to hide her eagerness. Bless Princess Ericka. She had promised to try to provide a piano for her.

"Feel free to play whenever you want," he said. "I hate to dump all this on you and leave so quickly, but I've got to get the palace construction schedule back on target. There's a cell phone for your use on the kitchen counter and a pad of paper with all the contact numbers, including emergency numbers, you may need. Hopefully you won't need the emergency numbers, but with young children, you never know." He paused and glanced first at Adelaide as she rubbed her eyes, and then he glanced down at Sam.

Gavin sighed, and the sweet sadness in all three faces clutched at Sara's heart.

"Are you sure you're ready for this? I don't know what you've been told, but we've been having a rough time lately."

"I've been briefed," she assured him. Determination coursed through her. She'd been put here for a reason. She would help this family find happiness and security again. It was her destiny. "I'm quite ready to care for your children. Now, move along to the palace. I'm sure they're waiting for you." She opened her arms to take Adelaide.

The baby stared at her suspiciously, but allowed Sara to hold her. "Come along, Sam. We're going to have juice and cookies. Give your father a big hug so he can have a good day at work. We all have our jobs to do. I'll need your help with Adelaide."

Gavin hugged Sam then grabbed a computer bag and headed for the door. "Call if you need anything."

"We'll be fine. Have a good day," she called, feeling a bit like the magical nannies she'd watched in old movies while she was growing up. She could do this, she told herself. Children were so sweet.

Suddenly Sara felt Adelaide clamp her teeth onto her collarbone with the force of a mini shark. Pain tore through her, and she couldn't swallow a surprised shriek. Adelaide pulled back at the sound and began to howl.

Sam kicked her in the shin.

Pain vibrated through her. Sara lost her breath. "Why did you do that?"

"You hurt my sister," he told her, crossing his arms over his chest.

"I didn't hurt her," Sara said over Adelaide's cries. "She bit me!"

Sam met her gaze for a long moment. "Oh. I think her mouth hurts. Can I have my juice and cookie?"

"First you must apologize for kicking me," she said as Adelaide's wails softened to moans.

"I'm sorry," he said reluctantly. "Can I—"

"Then you must make your request properly. May I please have juice and a cookie?"

He nodded. "Yes. You can."

Sara sighed. "Repeat after me. May I please have juice and a cookie?"

Sam relented and repeated her word for word.

"Well done," she said. "I'll get it for you right now."

Juggling Adelaide from one arm to the other, Sara

served Sam's snack at the table. Remembering she'd once had a toothache and that ice had seemed to help, she then returned to the refrigerator, pulled out an ice cube, wrapped it in a clean washcloth and offered it to Adelaide.

Silence followed. Five blessed seconds of silence. Sara took a deep breath as she watched Sam cram the cookie into his mouth and Adelaide gnaw on the cold washcloth. Maybe there was hope. But heaven help her, she couldn't serve juice and cookies all day.

It took far longer than it should have, but Sara crammed Adelaide in a stroller and retied Sam's shoes so they could go for a walk. She remembered as a child how much she'd craved being outside. Unlike the nannies she'd watched in movies, her nannies had kept her and her siblings inside the gloomy palace, which had always seemed to need repairs.

"Isn't it a beautiful day?" she said to Sam. "It's December, but it feels like May."

Sam just shrugged.

"Don't you enjoy being outside?" she asked.

He shrugged again. "I guess."

"I hear you lived in North Dakota. Isn't it very cold there?"

Sam nodded. "It snowed a lot. There's no snow here."

"Do you miss the snow?"

He shrugged. "I guess."

"What else do you miss?" she asked as she pushed the stroller.

A long silence followed. "Mommy," he finally whispered in a voice so low the wind almost carried it away.

Her heart contracted in sympathy and she squeezed Sam's shoulder. He immediately stiffened and drew back. *Too early for hugs*, she thought, making a mental note of it.

Several moments passed. "My dad keeps saying we can go to the beach, but we've only been once." Sam finally said.

Sara couldn't imagine taking both children to the beach, but perhaps she could enlist the help of someone. "Maybe we can do that soon. Just for a walk. The water may be too cool for a real swim."

Sam squinted his eyes up at her. "Yeah," he said skeptically.

Sara felt a ripple of challenge from that skeptical gaze. She frowned. "We'll go to the beach soon. You'll see."

Sam glanced down at the stroller. "Adelaide's asleep."

"Oh, heavens. We need to get her back to her crib," she said as she turned around.

"She'll wake up as soon as we get home."

"No. She won't," Sara insisted. "I just need to ease her into her crib."

"She's gonna wake up," Sam said, knowingly.

Turned out, Sam was right.

The rest of the day was a blur. Adelaide napped, but not for very long. Sam dozed. Sara served the children an early dinner and they were all half watching television as Gavin walked in the door. Sam immediately snapped to attention.

"How did your first day go with Sara?" Gavin asked.

Adelaide kicked her feet and howled. Sara gave her a washcloth to chew on.

"She took us for a walk," Sam said. "A long walk."

"Good," Gavin said and looked at Sara. "Everything okay?"

She moved her head in a circle because "okay" was relative. "Yes," she managed. "I figured out that Adelaide is teething."

Realization crossed his face. "Yeah. You're so right. I should have figured that out sooner."

"No problem," Sara said. "She'll just be chewing a cold washcloth for the first year of her life. Right, baby?" she said to Adelaide.

The baby frowned and chowed down on the washcloth.

"Good job," he said, then looked at Sam. "Time for us to go see Mr. Brahn."

Sam crossed his arms over his chest. "I don't wanna see Mr. Brahn."

Gavin glanced at Sara. "Mr. Brahn is a therapist. To help with the grief," he added in a low voice and walked toward Sam. "Hey, bud, we both need to go."

Sam stuck out his lower lip. "Mr. Brahn is boring. Don't wanna—"

"Ice cream or video game?" Sara whispered to Gavin.

Gavin glanced at her. "What?" he asked.

"Just a thought," she said. "Maybe after your appointment, you could do something fun."

He stood for a moment then nodded. "Good idea," he said then turned to Sam. "Ice cream or video game afterward?"

Sam's eyes lit up. "Can I have both?"

Gavin chuckled. "Only one," he said and scooped his son into his arms.

"Ice cream," Sam said.

Gavin sent a sideways glance at Sara. "This could make bedtime more difficult."

Sara smiled. "I'm sure Adelaide will be asleep by the

time you return, so it will be easier dealing with just one," she said, hoping that would be true. "If you need to know where to go, there's a wonderful gelato place downtown on Geneva Street."

"Geneva Gelato?" he asked.

"Yes," she said. "Have you been there?"

"No. Just sounded right," he said. "What flavor is the best?"

"The hazelnut chocolate is to die for. Best in the world, with the exception of Italy, of course," she said.

"You've traveled the whole world?" he asked, studying her.

His scrutiny made her nervous. She resisted biting her lip and shrugged her shoulders. "It's an expression. Try it and let me know what you think."

Sara watched the duo head out the door and turned to Adelaide. "How about a bath and a bottle?" she asked the baby, carrying her toward the kitchen sink. Princess Bridget of the royal Devereaux family had taken Sara under her wing so that Sara could learn some of the finer points of how to care for babies and active boys. Since Bridget had given birth to a baby girl less than a year ago and was the mother of two adopted boys, she was quite informed.

After cleaning the sink, Sara placed a towel in the bottom of it and filled it partway with warm water. She undressed Adelaide and put her into the bath. She tried to take the washcloth away from the baby, but Adelaide screamed in protest. "All right, all right. You can keep it. Let's just try not to get soap on it."

Sara talked the entire time about nothing in particular. Princess Bridget had told her that talking soothed and reassured infants while bathing. After the bath, she dried off Adelaide and dressed her in clean clothing and negotiated an exchange for a fresh washcloth.

Rechecking the schedule Gavin had given her, she saw that it was still too early for Adelaide's bottle and bedtime, so she attempted to read a book. Adelaide fussed and kicked in protest. "Not in the mood for reading," she muttered and walked around the house.

The sight of the piano jumped out at her. "Well, why not?" she asked. "The most you can do is howl at my playing."

Placing Adelaide in her infant rocker next to the piano, Sara sat down on the bench and looked down at the keyboard. A combination of excitement and relief snapped through her. Playing had been a solace for her for as long as she could remember.

She played a couple of scales to familiarize herself with the springiness of the keys and the tuning. Gavin had been correct. A few keys were off, but she was so happy to play she didn't care. "I know Mozart is supposed to be good for kids, but I'm going to play it safe with Bach. I'm sure you'll let me know your thoughts on Bach's *Goldberg Variations*."

Sara played and since no screaming commenced, she continued for fifteen minutes. When she stopped and turned to glance at Adelaide, the baby was sitting calmly and seemed to have forgotten the need for her washcloth. Sara smiled and picked up the baby from the carrier. "Good girl. Bach has been soothing the savage beast in all of us for many years. Time for your bottle."

Adelaide drank her formula, Sara rocked her for a few minutes, then placed the baby in her crib. She made sure the baby monitor was turned on and walked quietly from the room. Exhaustion hit her and she let out a heavy sigh. She realized this was only the first day of being a nanny, but she hadn't expected the job to completely sap her energy. What a wimp. It was just eight o'clock and more than anything, she wanted to go to bed.

Instead, she poured herself a cup of tea and sat on the couch, blinking her eyes so she would stay awake.

Gavin ushered Sam in the door of the cottage. They'd returned much later than he'd intended, but the palace had ordered road construction on a twenty-four-hour basis. Despite the limited population of the Mediterranean island, there'd been a ton of traffic tonight.

Sam proudly carried the small white bag holding a cup of mostly melted gelato for Sara. He darted toward the den and skidded to a halt. He glanced up at Gavin. "She's fast asleep," Sam said in a loud whisper, using the language from some of the books Gavin and his mother had read to him.

Gavin gazed at the new nanny to his children and felt a shot of sympathy. He could understand her exhaustion. Between Sam's fear of new people and Adelaide's general crankiness, he'd wondered if he should ask for two nannies instead of one. He stepped closer to Sara, taking in the sight of her. Faint blue circles shadowed her eyes, but her skin was like ivory porcelain. Her dark eyelashes spread like fans under her closed eyelids and a heavy strand of her dark hair covered one eye. Her pink lips parted slightly, almost as if in invitation.

Her body was slim, but hinted at the warm curves of a woman. A thud of awareness settled in his gut, startling him. He shook it off. Heaven knew he had no room for those kinds of thoughts. His kids needed him and he needed to get himself centered. Gavin and his late wife had grown apart during the past couple of years. They'd tried to put things back together—that was how Adelaide had happened. But he'd been concerned when Lauren had gotten pregnant again because she'd suffered from postpartum depression after she'd given birth to Sam. Even though he knew Lauren's death had been an accident, he still couldn't shake his feeling of guilt. He wasn't sure he ever would.

Sam nervously clutched the paper bag between his hands. Sara's eyes fluttered at the sound and she glanced up at both of them. She winced and straightened. "Oh, no. I fell asleep. What time is it?"

Gavin glanced at his watch. "Ten after eight," he said.

"Oh," she said, laughing. "Eight-minute nap. Ten at the most. Welcome back. Shall I pour you some tea?" she asked Gavin. "Would you like something to drink, Sam?"

"I'm not a big tea drinker," Gavin said. "We'll both take water. Sam has something for you."

Sara looked at Sam and saw the paper bag he held. She smiled and clapped her hands together. "Oh, don't tell me what it is. Let me guess," she said. "Is it pizza?"

Sam shook his head.

"Is it cheese and crackers?"

Sam shook his head.

"Is it a bunny?"

Sam shook his head and his little mouth lifted in a grin. "Here," he said, offering the bag to her.

She opened the bag and pulled out the small cup of gelato and took off the top. She dipped her head and took a swipe with her tongue. "Hazelnut. My favorite. Thank you so much. What kind did you have?"

"Chocolate and marshmallow," Sam said.

"I took your advice and got the hazelnut. You were right. It's pretty good. You'd probably better eat that quickly. We got caught in road construction, so it's melted."

"Just nice and soft. Let me get your water," she said as she headed for the kitchen.

As soon as she left, Sam turned to him. "She's pretty, but she's a terrible guesser."

Gavin couldn't shut off his awareness of her presence. It wasn't all bad. She smiled easily and something about her made everything feel a little less dark and gloomy. She talked with Sam even though he rarely gave her a verbal response.

"Go to bed," Gavin told her although it was early. "Tomorrow's another day."

She nodded. "So it is. Shall I put Sam to bed?"

Gavin shook his head. "No. That's my treat. I'll take the first middle-of-the-night wake-up, but I'd appreciate it if you would take the second."

Her eyes widened. "Two wake-ups?"

He shrugged. "We're still adjusting."

"Then I'll try to be ready. Good night, Sam. Thank you for the delicious gelato."

Sam nodded and Gavin nudged his son. "Say you're welcome."

"You're welcome," Sam echoed in a small voice.

"Sweet sleep to both of you," she said, and then she left the room.

Sometime when it was dark, Sam awakened. He felt panic overtake him. His heart raced. He glanced toward the cartoon night-light and took a deep breath.

He took more deep breaths and thought about his mother. She had left, then never come home again. He missed her so much. He didn't want to lose anyone else.

Sliding out of his bed, he silently scampered to his father's room. The door wasn't closed all the way. Sam pushed it open and went inside. His father was on his back, softly snoring.

Sam felt a sliver of relief. He watched his father for several more moments. Then he wandered down the hall to the new nanny's bedroom. Her door was also open. He wandered inside and saw her sleeping on her side. He heard an odd sound. It took a moment for him to figure out what it was.

The ocean. Waves. He loved that sound.

He loved the sound so much he wanted to hear it more. He decided to lie down on the carpet. Sam wished he had a blanket, but he liked the sound more than he missed his blanket.

As the swooshing sound continued, he calmed down and felt droopy and sleepy. He didn't remember when he fell asleep.

Sara awakened to an unfamiliar sound. She heard a series of humming and grunting sounds and frowned as she shifted in her bed. Staring into the darkness, she saw a small figure on her floor. It took a moment for her to figure out who it was. Sam.

Sliding from her bed, she picked him up and held him against her. He startled.

"It's okay. I'm your nanny. Sara," she said, walking toward his room.

"But—"

Gavin appeared in the hallway. "What happened? I usually find him sleeping on the floor of my bedroom."

"He was in my bedroom."

Gavin gathered his son into his arms. "What's up, bud?"

"I liked the waves," he said.

Gavin looked at her curiously.

"My sound machine," Sara said. "I keep it on an ocean setting." She looked toward Sam and stroked his forehead. "Would you like to hear the waves at night?"

He nodded.

"Done," she said. Then she went and moved her sound machine to Sam's bedroom.

With his hands on his hips, Gavin stood looking at his son. *Protecting his son*, she thought. His stance tugged at her heart. She couldn't remember a time she'd awakened to the sight of her father watching over her. *Stop*, she told herself, closing her eyes. Her life was all about now and the future. No whining about the past.

Taking a deep breath, she opened her eyes and found Gavin staring at her. He crooked a finger at her and pointed toward the hallway. She followed him outside the door of Sam's bedroom.

"That's a first," Gavin said. "For six months Sam has been coming into my bedroom and staring at me, making sure I'm not going to leave him forever. The way, in his eyes, his mother did."

Her heart twisted at his words. "He's had a hard time. You've all had a hard time."

Gavin gave a slow nod, and she was all too aware of his height, his power, his masculinity. "Yeah, we have. Who would have known a sound machine would make such a difference?"

She shrugged, knowing that the sound machine was her secret to a good night's sleep. "Yeah. Who would have known?"

"Thank you," he said, lowering his head toward hers.

She caught her breath.

He squeezed her arm. "Get some sleep."

Sara nearly collapsed in a combination of relief and strange disappointment. She stared after him and felt a flip in her stomach. Yes, she definitely needed more sleep.

Hours later, she heard the sound of Gavin's voice. She immediately sat up in her bed. His voice was coming from the nursery. She glanced at the clock in her room. Seven thirty.

Sara leaped from her bed and ran into the nursery. "Problems?" she asked. "I can't believe I slept this late."

Gavin, still wearing pajamas, was changing Adelaide's diaper. "She hasn't slept this long in forever. She wet through her diaper to her sheets."

"Oops," she said.

Gavin shrugged. "It's a good problem. Did you do something different with her bedtime routine?"

"I played a little Bach on the piano," she said.

Gavin glanced at her. "Must have worked."

She shrugged. "We can hope."

"Yeah," he said.

"Can I take a quick shower?"

"Sure," he said. "You're due that after the past twenty-four hours."

Sara grabbed a quick shower, rubbed herself dry and wrapped her hair in a towel for two minutes. Pulling on her clothes, she ditched the towel and pulled her hair into a wet knot at the back of the neck, all the while resolving to take her bath at night. She'd just been too tired last night.

Racing into the kitchen, she smiled her best smile. "I'm here for duty," she said.

Three pairs of brown eyes stared back at her full of hope, fear and expectation.

"All right. Let's get going."

"You're a brave woman," Gavin said. He was dressed to head out the door. "Or crazy," he muttered as he handed Adelaide over to her. "Just tell me you'll last the week."

Sara blinked. "Week? I thought this was at least a two- or three-month assignment."

"Yes. Of course. Three months," Gavin said. "Call me if you need me," he added as he headed out the door.

"But you don't really want me to call you, do you?" she said.

He paused just before he closed the door behind him. "Truth..." he said, turning around to face her. "I'm grateful for all you've already done. Call me for anything."

Her heart took a strange twist and turn. He was a great father. Maybe even a great human being.

Chapter Two

Sara fed the kids, then secured them into child safety seats in her car. Sam attended preschool three days each week and this was one of his designated days. She'd also prepared a snack for him to eat.

Driving toward the small building, she got into the short car line.

"I don't like preschool," Sam said.

Sara glanced at him from the rearview mirror. "What's not to like? You get to play and meet other children. You get to make things and eat a snack."

"I don't like my teacher," he said. "She's mean."

"Mean," Sara echoed. "What do you mean she's mean? Does she hit you?"

"No," he said reluctantly. "She won't leave me alone. Sometimes I don't want to play with everyone else."

"You can play by yourself when you get home. Preschool is good for you. It's only for a few hours. Maybe you can help someone else who is having a bad day," she said in the most firm, positive nanny voice she could muster. "I'll be back to pick you up before you know it."

She wanted to give him a hug and kiss but knew he wasn't interested in her affection. Just her sound machine, so far, she thought wryly.

Sara returned home with Adelaide and attempted to get more settled in to her bedroom. She called her sister to check on her, but the call went straight to voice mail. Who knew what her sister was up to? Tabitha was working as a hostess at an exclusive restaurant until the Devereaux family could help find a more suitable position for her.

Tabitha had seemed more than a bit restless lately, and that worried Sara. Their brother, Alex, had persuaded them to leave their home country for safety concerns. He'd assured them he would meet them in Chantaine, but he was nowhere to be found. Tabitha hadn't tolerated any sort of restraints on her activities very well in the past and she'd been known to act impulsively. Sara hoped Tabitha would be able to keep herself under control a little longer.

Closing her eyes for a moment, Sara took a deep breath and tried to shake off her worries. There was little she could do about Tabitha since they weren't supposed to be seen together, and there was nothing she could do about her brother. She needed to focus on the present. Who knew what the future would bring?

She picked up Sam from preschool and he presented her with a note from the teacher. Sara decided to pass it along to Gavin later and tried to converse with Sam to no avail. After asking ten questions and trying several times to start a conversation, she decided to shut up. Maybe Sam was decompressing.

Just as she pulled into the driveway, she heard Sam's heavy sigh. "Everyone is talking about Christmas," he said in a grumbly voice.

"Well, it's that time of year. We'll need to get a tree and decorate soon."

"Bet Daddy won't want one," he said.

Sara looked at Sam in surprise. "Why not?"

"He doesn't want to do anything fun," Sam muttered. "Can I go inside?"

"Of course," she said, and she unbuckled his seat belt.

In contrast to the previous day, the afternoon passed quietly. The part-time housekeeper and cook arrived to clean and prepare meals. Janece Dillon, a lovely middle-aged woman, prepared several meals to freeze for later. "So, you're the new nanny," Janece said. "You look so young."

"Thank you. That's what Mr. Sinclair said to me. I'm actually twenty-seven," she said.

"Well, I hope you'll be able to stay around for the sake of the mister and his little ones," she said.

"What do you mean?" Sara asked, carrying Adelaide on her hip.

"Well, there have been quite a few," Janece said as she stirred a pot of pasta sauce. "Nannies, that is. Poor man and his children have been through so much."

Sara hadn't been told there'd been several previous nannies. That must be why Gavin had expressed hope that she would make it through the week.

That evening after Gavin arrived home, she slipped him the note from Sam's teacher. "I didn't read it," she said.

He opened the note and sighed, raking his hand

through his hair. "I don't know what to do. He hates going for therapy. He doesn't like preschool. I feel like we're not making any progress with him."

"It hasn't been that long," she said. "Just six months, right?"

"But he's four years old and he hardly ever smiles," he said.

"He smiled when you took him for ice cream," she said, wanting to encourage him.

He looked at her and chuckled. "That's not something I can do every night."

"True," she said. "But we can figure out other things. His favorite foods. Maybe a pet would help."

"A pet?" he echoed. "I'm barely surviving with these two. Add in an animal and I'll have to wave a white flag."

She shrugged. "I wasn't allowed pets when I was a child. Except one of my nannies allowed me to sneak in a few visits with her hamster, Willie. That was a lot of fun."

"Why so many nannies?" he asked. "I can't imagine you causing a lot of trouble, although most of us can't resist getting into trouble every now and then."

"I didn't," she said. Was that a hint of a sexy glint in his eye? Or was she imagining it? "I stayed out of trouble. My sister and brother, though, made up for me."

"Is your family originally from Chantaine?" he asked.

"No. We're from the mainland, but my parents did a lot of traveling," she said. Uncomfortable with the curiosity she glimpsed in his gaze, she waved toward the stove. "Janece left a pot of pasta and sauce for dinner tonight. Sam has wandered in here a few times, but I thought you might like to eat together."

"That will work, and it's one of his favorite meals," he said. "I'll wash up, change clothes and help serve it."

"I can serve it," she said. "I just don't possess advanced cooking skills."

"Me neither," he said. "That's why a part-time cook and housekeeper was part of my package of compensation for this job. And a nanny," he said, meeting her gaze. "The children may not show it yet, but we're glad you're here to help."

"Speaking of helping, we need to think about celebrating the holidays. Sam mentioned that everyone at preschool is talking about Christmas."

Gavin raked his hand through his hair. "I haven't really been in the mood for Christmas."

"Well, you can't just ignore it," she said. "Children love Christmas."

"Maybe we should keep it low-key this year," he said.

"Sam mentioned that he didn't think you would want decorations," she said.

"He may be right. Besides, we left our decorations in storage in the States."

"He also said you don't want to do fun things anymore. It's not my place to tell you how you should act, but perhaps if he saw that you could enjoy some aspects of life, then maybe he would feel free to do so, also."

Gavin stared at her for a long moment. "You're right. It's not your place to tell me how to act."

Sara felt his assertion for her to step back. *Yes, sir*, she thought. Adelaide let out a squawk from her infant seat. She'd been snoozing and now clearly wanted to be entertained. "Dinner may take a few more minutes.

I suspect the queen of the house will need her diaper changed and she doesn't like to wait. Can't say I blame her," said Sara.

After dinner, Sara took Sam and Adelaide for a walk down the street while Gavin worked on the palace construction project for a bit. "A beautiful evening for a walk, isn't it, Sam?"

Sam shrugged and stuck his hands in his pockets. "I wanted to play my video game."

"You can do that tomorrow. The sun is still shining, so we should take advantage. Getting outside is good for you. I always loved getting outside when I was a child."

Sam glanced up at her and sighed. "Did you have video games?"

"Not that I remember," she said. "I had a piano and my house always seemed dark." Sara glanced at Adelaide and noticed the baby's eyes were closed. "Oh, no, Adelaide is falling asleep. Help me keep her awake so she'll sleep through the night." Sara thought a minute, then began to sing. "Two little blackbirds sitting on a hill. One named Jack. One named Jill." She wiggled her finger on the handle of the stroller. "Fly away Jack. Fly away Jill. Now your turn," she said.

Sam gave her a blank look.

"Surely you've played this game before. It's been around forever."

Sam shrugged.

"Two little blackbirds sitting in the snow. One named Fast. One named—" She broke off and waited and waited. And waited. "One named Fast. One named Ssss—"

"Snake?" he said. Sara smiled.

"One named Fast. One named Slow," she said and

continued the rhyme. "Two little blackbirds soaring in the sky. One named Low. One named?" She glanced at him expectantly. "It needs to rhyme with sky."

"High," he finally said, and Sara spotted a twinge of triumph in his eyes.

"High," she said. "Say it louder so we keep Adelaide awake."

Sam yelled the word and Adelaide gave a start, blinking her eyes. "Good job. Two little blackbirds..."

They played the game for the rest of the walk. She hadn't heard Sam speak so much since she'd started working with the family, and although she couldn't exactly call it conversation, it counted as interaction. She planned to put Adelaide on her tummy on a blanket to get her moving a bit. Hopefully both children would sleep well after the exercise. Princess Bridget had told her that one of the keys to parent and child happiness was to wear out the children, and Sara was taking that child-care tip to heart. Trouble was she wondered if she would last through the evening herself.

In fact, after she washed her face and brushed her teeth, she took a book with her to her room and fell asleep midpage. She awakened in the middle of the night, her book resting on her chest and the light from the lamp making her squint her eyes. Reaching for the cup of water she liked to keep on the bedside table, she realized she'd forgotten to bring a cup last night.

Not wanting to awaken Sam by going into the adjoining bathroom, she tiptoed from her room and down the dark hallway. She poured herself a cup of water and drank most of it, then turned off the light at the kitchen sink and slowly made her way down the hall.

She bumped into something that wasn't a wall. Panic

rushed through her. A squeak escaped her throat and she nearly dropped her cup.

"It's me," Gavin said before he swore under his breath, probably from the water she spilled on him. "What?

"I am carrying a cup of water," she said, trying to catch her breath, caught in an unexpected swirl of emotions and sensations. He felt so strong and sure against her. He was holding her to keep her from falling. She couldn't remember the last time someone had held her other than her family. "You startled me."

"I heard a noise and thought it might be Sam," he said, still holding her in his arms.

She felt so safe. His strength vibrated throughout her. Clinging to him, she felt a surprising mix of awareness and emotion thrum through her.

Still struggling for balance, she leaned against him. She inhaled his scent and nearly fell. "Sorry," she managed. "I didn't mean to pour water on you."

"Could be worse," he said, still holding her.

Sara wanted him to keep holding her. She wanted this feeling never to end. Where were these thoughts coming from?

"Yes," she said. She still clung to him, soaking him up.

The moment stretched between them. "You okay?" he finally asked her.

"Yes," she said reluctantly.

"You sure?"

She took another deep breath and inhaled his scent again. "Yes," she whispered.

He gradually stepped away from her, releasing her from his embrace.

In the darkness, she was caught off guard by the

strange stirring in her stomach. Was this desire? "I'll go back to bed," she managed.

"What about your water?" he asked.

"I'll be fine," she said, and forced herself to back away from him as much as she could when she really wanted to stay close to him.

"Good night, then," he said in a husky masculine voice that raced through her bloodstream.

Why was he affecting her this way?

"Good night," she said and stumbled to her bedroom. Her heart pounded in her chest. She felt something she hadn't felt in a long time.

Sara didn't know what to do with the strange sensation. She'd pushed her wants aside for too long. Sara sank onto her bed and closed her eyes. The room spun. This wasn't at all convenient. Perhaps it was all an aberration and would disappear in the morning. She couldn't want the father of the children she was caring for. It just wouldn't work.

Taking several deep breaths, she wished she could also drink some water to calm herself. Instead, she took more deep breaths, telling herself that she wasn't attracted to Gavin. She absolutely could not and did not want him.

Her heart still racing, Sara counted backward from three hundred and prayed she would fall asleep before she reached one.

During the next few days, she avoided Gavin as much as she could, which was difficult due to the small size of the cottage. Despite her best efforts, he brushed against her or she bumped against him. Each time it happened, she felt as if she had received an electrical shock. She felt increasingly aware of his body. Bloody inconvenient. When she crawled into bed at night, she should have been exhausted, and she was. When she closed her eyes, however, crazy images filled her mind. What would it be like to be held in his strong arms? What if, for once, she could let down her guard and relish the protectiveness of a man? She wondered what his mouth would feel like if he kissed her.

Sara groaned and frowned at herself. *Stop it.* At the same time her contrary mind nudged her. Could she even remember the last time she'd been kissed?

Nine days after she'd started her position, she put Adelaide to bed and went to the kitchen to get her cup of water. She didn't want to make the mistake of running into Gavin again in the dark. Just as she left the kitchen, he approached her.

Sara almost spilled her cup of water even though there was plenty of light.

"You don't have to run off to your room every night. You're welcome to use the other rooms in the house. You can watch television," Gavin said.

"That's okay, thank you. I've been reading in the evenings. I have headphones and I also often listen to music," she said, wishing she didn't feel so aware of him.

"I guess you're ready for some peace by the time the kids are in bed," he said, rubbing his chin thoughtfully. "I wasn't sure you would last. It's not exactly a plum position for a woman like you."

"Why would you say that?"

"Don't get me wrong. You're good with the kids, but this just doesn't seem like your regular line of work."

"I needed a change," she said. "As you saw from my résumé, I apprenticed as a nanny for Princess Bridget's children. I may not be as experienced as some, but I like to think I make up for what I lack in compassion and determination."

"I wasn't criticizing you," he said. "You're just prettier than I expected."

Sara blinked. His compliment caught her off guard. She'd received compliments from many people before, but they'd all known of her position, and frankly she'd never been sure if there'd been a hidden agenda or not. Struggling with a combination of self-consciousness and pleasure, she cleared her throat. "Thank you very much."

"Besides, you and I both know the kids are at a tough age. Between Adelaide and her teething and Sam's situation..."

"I think Sam is tolerating me now," she said, feeling a twitch of humor when she thought about how he sighed when she engaged him with silly games. "Adelaide likes to be fed on time and soothed when she's hurting. I honestly hadn't even considered leaving." Actually, she didn't know if she had that choice. She'd agreed to work in anonymity in exchange for her and her sister's safety.

"That's good to hear. However, you haven't had a day off and you're due. I may be able to arrange backup care during the week later on, but it would help if you would pick a weekend day."

"Okay," she said, feeling a sliver of relief. Perhaps it would help her perspective and clear her mind to have a day away. She was also determined to visit her sister who had not responded to her calls or text messages recently. "Saturday."

He nodded. "That will work. If you need anything, let me know."

"I will," she said, the intensity in his eyes tugging at something inside her. "Good night, then," she said, and she and quickly strode to her room. Her heart was pounding too quickly. She felt flushed. Sara swore under her breath. She couldn't wait for Saturday.

Anticipating a surprise visit with her sister, Sara drove into town and parked on the street. She bought some fresh fruit and carried it up the steps to Tabitha's apartment. Spotting the wreath on her sister's door, she felt a rush of approval as she knocked. At least Tabitha was giving a nod to the holidays. Sara waited. And waited.

She knocked on the door again and Tabitha finally answered the door, wearing a gown she'd clearly donned in a haphazard fashion. Her eyes were droopy from a late sleep-in. "Hi," Tabitha said in a fake cheery voice.

"Hi," Sara returned. "I've called you, but didn't hear back. I brought you fruit. I like your wreath."

Tabitha gave a half smile. "It's the least I can do. I'm trying to muster a little seasonal joy. It wouldn't be good to snarl at the guests at the restaurant just because this is another Christmas I'll be spending trapped. Thank you for the fruit," she said, taking the fruit. "This is a tricky time..."

A handsome man appeared behind her. "Want to introduce me?" he asked.

"Of course," Tabitha said. "My sis—" She broke off. "My good friend, Sara. This is Christoph."

"Pleasure to meet you," Christoph said. "I'll take a shower while you two visit."

The man who resembled Adonis disappeared down the hall with a towel draped around his waist. Sara gaped at Tabitha. "What on earth are you doing with him?"

"Having a little fun," she said. "He's amazing in bed. Why should I deprive myself? He doesn't know my real name."

"How do you know that?" Sara demanded.

"He thinks I'm just a highly educated hostess," Tabitha said. "Oh, wait. That's what I really am at the moment."

"Do you wish you were back in Sergenia?" Sara asked. "Worrying about being kidnapped?"

"I didn't worry all that much," Tabitha said. She sighed. "Oh, give me a break, Sasha—Sara, you've got to admit this arrangement is entirely too constraining."

"We're fortunate the Devereaux family agreed to allow us to stay here," she reminded Tabitha.

"You've always been the one to deny your needs. I can't do that, and you really shouldn't. It's not good for you."

Sara stared at her younger sister. "There's a difference between delaying gratification and denying needs."

Tabitha shrugged her shoulders. "Sounds the same to me. Am I supposed to sit in a dark corner here until someone says it's safe to come out?" Tabitha shook her head. "I'm young. I want to live."

"Well, just be careful," Sara said. "Things can happen…during sex."

Tabitha laughed but squeezed Sara's arm. "How

would you know?" she asked. She immediately became contrite. "I'm sorry. It must be hard being the family saint. You've made it easy for me to be the sinner."

Sara drew Tabitha into her arms, tightly embracing her younger sister. "I worry about you. I don't want you to suffer."

Tabitha's gaze softened. "I'm not in pain when Christoph is around. He's Greek. He makes me feel happy. He makes me forget my troubles."

Sara still felt uneasy about Tabitha's lover. "If you say so," she said. "I just want you to be safe, careful and happy."

"In our situation, one out of three isn't so bad," Tabitha said.

Sara took a deep breath. "Look after yourself. I'll call you. Try to respond," she said.

Tabitha smiled. "I'll do my best. Are you sure you don't want a cup of tea?"

Sara shook her head. "I think I heard the water in the shower turn off. Time for me to go. Call me," she said, kissing her sister on the cheek before she walked out of the apartment.

Sara wandered around downtown, glancing into shop windows even though she was distracted. She stopped by the gelato shop, ordered her favorite hazelnut gelato and headed for the beach. It was early December and although it was too chilly for swimming, she wanted to make the most of her day. Spooning the delicious dessert into her mouth, she stared at the beautiful azure ocean and felt completely lost.

She was full of worry over her brother, who had been missing for months, and her sister, who appeared determined to compensate for the constraints of the past several months. Sara sighed and her mind wandered to Gavin, Sam and Adelaide. A little trip to the beach would mean so much to all of them.

Spooning the last bit of gelato into her mouth, Sara stood and brushed the sand off her backside. So much for escaping Gavin and his brood. It appeared that her own family situation was crazier than his.

Gavin alternated between encouraging Sam to eat his lunch and spooning mushy green peas into Adelaide's mouth. She banged the extra spoon he'd given her on the tray of the high chair. The sound of metal repeatedly striking plastic reminded him of a bad visit to the dentist.

Sam appeared to be having a glum day. "Hey, bud," he said to his son. "Eat a few more bites of your sandwich."

Gavin gave Adelaide another bite and she spit the green matter back at him, chortling in delight and banging the tray. "Hey. Give your poor dad a break."

At that moment, Gavin heard the front door open and footsteps. He glanced up to find Sara in the doorway and felt a shot of relief. "You're back early," he said.

He felt her gaze wander over him. She bit her lip as if to contain her amusement. "I'm delighted to know I'm not the only one on whom she likes to shower her food."

"I bet you look better in green than I do," he said, somehow feeling much lighter. He wiped Adelaide's face. She screeched at him in return. "Hope your morning was better than ours."

"Not bad," she said. "I ate gelato and sat on the beach for a little while."

"Gelato," Gavin echoed.

"The beach," Sam said, jealousy oozing from his tone.

Sara glanced at both of them. "There's nothing preventing us from taking a little trip to the beach," she said. "We don't even have to swim. We just need to slather on some sunscreen, throw on a hat and roll up our pants if we dare to have the chilly water on our toes."

Sam scrambled up on his knees in his chair and stared hopefully in Gavin's face. "Can we go, Daddy? Can we?"

Gavin had so rarely seen Sam exhibit this much enthusiasm during the past few months. There was only one answer he could give his son.

Chapter Three

Sam zoomed along the sandy beach. When the water was calm, he stepped into it up to his ankles.

"I can't believe he's tolerating the chilly water so well," Sara said.

"You forget that he spent the past several years playing in the snows of North Dakota," Gavin said.

Adelaide wiggled inside the baby carrier strapped to Gavin's chest and kicked her chubby little legs. She was almost too big for it, but they'd left in a rush and since she was putting everything in her mouth, he suspected there was no way he'd be able to keep her from ingesting sand, shells and rocks.

"Adelaide really wants free, doesn't she?" Sara said, smiling as her hair blew in the breeze.

"Yeah. I'm just not prepared to dig sand out of her mouth," he said. "Trust me. It would be a real mood killer."

Sara nodded and closed her eyes as she lifted her head. "The ocean makes everything better."

"Unless it involves a tsunami or hurricane," he said.

"Feeling a little cynical?" she asked.

Yeah, he thought, but didn't say it aloud. Instead he took a deep breath of the salt-scented air and then another. He felt his insides stretch open a bit. Gavin had felt tight and stiff for a long time. He'd had to stay tight in order to hold everything together. Everything had been so sad. His kids had lost their mother. His wife had lost her life. He had no right to breathe easy. He had no right to even a moment of happiness. Taking another breath, he almost felt a little sore at the expansion of his lungs.

"Maybe we should step into the water like Sam," she encouraged. "Maybe it will make us feel better."

"You make it sound like a baptism," he said.

"Maybe it is," she said. She took off her shoes and barely stepped into the water. She let out a little squeal and glanced over her shoulder. "Give me a minute to get used to it."

Gavin watched her take a few more steps into the water. She was an odd combination of characteristics. Pretty in a quiet way, she looked young for her years. At the same time, he saw glimpses of an old soul in her eyes. Gavin smirked at himself. Old soul. Was he getting poetic about the nanny?

Shaking off his dour attitude, he ditched his shoes and walked toward Sam and Sara. He stepped into the water and felt the initial shock of the chill. He waited for the magic. No dramatic wave rushed through him. He just felt a little lighter.

"It's strange, but it feels good, doesn't it?" Sara said more than asked.

"I guess," he said. "Sam, you're not getting drenched, are you?"

"No," Sam said, but he kept wandering farther into the water.

"Don't go any farther," Gavin called. "You might step into a hole. I don't want you going in over your head."

"Okay," Sam said, walking in circles and staring at his feet.

"He loves it," Sara said. "I'd like to bring him down here more often, but I'm not sure I could watch both of them at the same time."

Gavin nodded. "I'll try to make more time for it. It definitely takes two adults with these kids. So when did you fall in love with the ocean?"

"I grew up in a landlocked region, but we often took vacations on the shore. It was one of the few times we could count on being with our parents. Although there was always a nanny or two along."

"Sounds like you didn't spend much time with your parents when you were growing up," he said, curious about her background.

"I didn't," she said, crossing her arms over her chest. "My father's business required a lot of social engagements, so my parents traveled more than they stayed home."

"Hmm," he said. "What about sports games and programs at school? Did they show up for those events?"

She shrugged. "Occasionally. We were always cared for, but we were also raised to be independent. But enough about—" She broke off. "Sam!"

Panic rushed through him. Gavin glanced in the direction of his son. He'd barely taken his eyes off him, but Sam was now up to his shoulders in the water. Gavin ran toward his son with Sara rushing beside him. He grabbed one of Sam's arms and pulled him closer to shore.

"I told you not to go any farther into the ocean," Gavin scolded, his heart hammering.

"I wanted to be in the waves," Sam said. "I didn't get my face wet."

"One more step and you could have," Gavin said.

Sam hung his head. "I'm sorry."

Sara squeezed Sam's shoulder. "Of course you are. And I'm sure you'll be more careful next time. You don't want to frighten your father and me. The ocean can be tricky even for experienced swimmers. Have you had swimming lessons?"

Sam shook his head.

Sara met Gavin's gaze. "Perhaps we can add that to the schedule."

Gavin nodded. "Good idea. I should have thought of it before now."

"You've had a lot on your mind. But even after your swimming lessons, you always need to have a buddy," she said firmly. She then gave both Gavin and Sam a once-over.

He couldn't resist returning the favor. Her rolled-up jeans were plastered to her body and the shirt under her jacket had gotten a big splash, making it transparent. He would have to be blind not to notice the little lacy bra she wore and the way her nipples pressed against the light covering. The sight grabbed at his gut and lower. He felt an odd rumble of awareness and want.

It had been a long time since he'd allowed himself to get aroused, and he wasn't going to start today, he told himself. He tore his gaze from her body, but an unwelcome restlessness still rippled through him and his mouth watered with the forbidden idea of tasting her, starting with her lips and working all the way down the rest of her body.

"We weren't prepared for a full-out swim today, but it looks like we got one anyway," she said with a wry laugh.

"Can't disagree. Next time we'll be better prepared," he said, but he couldn't help wondering how he was going to rein in his imagination if Sara was wearing a bathing suit instead of being fully clothed.

Sara gave Adelaide a bath and put the baby in her crib with a few toys while Gavin helped Sam with his shower. Afterward, she managed a quick shower, too. Piling her damp hair on her head, Sara picked up Adelaide and headed for the kitchen.

Gavin was heating soup and grilling sandwiches. "I'm not that good in the kitchen, but I make a mean grilled cheese."

"Ah, American comfort food," she said, nodding.

"How did you know?" he asked.

"I once had an American nanny," she said. "I also learned about peanut butter and jelly from her, although European peanut butter doesn't compare to the American version."

"Tell me about it," Gavin said. "I should have stocked up before we came to Chantaine."

"So true. Shall I help? I can stir the soup," she said, thinking how attractive he looked standing next to the stove with his ruffled hair and broad shoulders. He wasn't nearly as refined as the men with whom she usually spent time, although heaven knew she hadn't had much time to spend with anyone. She'd been dedicated to piano perfection from such an early age. Her parents and royal advisors had told her the country would always be proud of her abilities and performances.

So much for that. She and her siblings had been tossed aside like rubbish. Sara wondered if she should have tried for a career in engineering. Much more practical, she supposed.

Thoughts about her country made her feel troubled and itchy inside. She wiggled her fingers. Music had always provided her with solace. "I haven't noticed music around the house. I have music stored on my cell phone, but no speakers."

"Speakers," he echoed as if it were a foreign concept.

"You have children," she said, unable to edit herself. "Children need music."

He blinked. "I hadn't thought about it. I'll get some speakers," he said as he reached for his phone. "I'll write a message to myself."

Sara's heart softened. Maybe she shouldn't have been so adamant. "Perhaps, I could play something on the piano in the meantime. I may be a little rusty, though," she warned him.

Gavin glanced at her and nodded. "Yeah. That would be great."

Sara went to the den and ran her fingers over the keys, then she began to play an upbeat elementary piece by Bach—Minuet in G. She played until the end and found Sam standing beside the piano staring at her. Up to this point, she'd been so busy when both children had been in the house that she hadn't played for Sam. "A little Beethoven? How about "Ode to Joy"? Much better with a full orchestra, but I'll do my best," she said as she started playing the piece.

Aware of several blunders, she soldiered through and took a deep breath.

She turned and found Sam and Gavin, who was holding Adelaide, staring at her in amazement. "I thought you said you'd taken a few lessons."

"I did," she said. "Was it that bad?"

Gavin shook his head and chuckled. "*Bad* was not a word that came to mind. Are you sure you're not a professional?"

Sara shrugged. "In the arts, the word *professional* is relative. I'm far from the best." She smiled. "You enjoyed it?"

"I did," Gavin said. Adelaide kicked in approval. "Adelaide did. What about you, Sam?"

Sam stared at Sara as if she'd suddenly gained magical powers. Or a third head. He glanced at the piano, then at her. Then he nodded.

"Time for dinner?" Sara asked, wanting to divert attention away from herself.

Gavin nodded and grinned, oozing a masculine charm that made her feel a strange tingle inside. "I didn't burn the sandwiches."

Sara fed Adelaide carrots while she, Gavin and Sam munched on their sandwiches, soup and chips. It was a meal mostly devoid of nutrition, but satisfying. Adelaide spit out a spoonful of carrots, but it only hit the tray.

"Yes, Your Highness, we are done," Sara said and put the carrots aside. "We must all learn from our mistakes, and strained peas are the worst," she said to Gavin.

He shot her a look of commiseration.

Sara squeezed Adelaide's sweet cheeks and the baby smiled. "She's clearly not underfed," Sara said, then met Gavin's gaze. "You're a good father."

Gavin took a swift breath. "That's debatable."

"Not by me," she said. She wiped off Adelaide's face. "Would you like to give your princess a bottle and put her to bed tonight? Sam and I can read."

"Good idea," Gavin said. "Thank you for coming home early."

Sara took Sam to the den and read the same book three times. Sam kept eyeing the piano, but Sara thought she should keep the house quiet since it was bedtime. She read the same book again and Gavin came to collect his son.

"Ready for bed, big guy?" he asked.

Sam jumped up from the sofa and leaped into Gavin's arms. Sara sighed as Gavin carried his son to bed.

Sara usually went to bed when the children did, but this time she put in her earbuds and listened to music while she rested on the sofa. Moments later, Gavin appeared, sitting beside her.

She inhaled his clean, masculine scent and decided it was a bit intoxicating. "Hi," she said, pulling out her earbuds. "Did Sam settle down?"

"He settles down much more easily since you donated your sound machine," he said.

"I'm glad it helped him," she said, thinking of how she missed the waves, but she wouldn't tell Gavin that.

"We swiped it from you," he said. "I keep intending to get you a replacement."

"No problem," she said, and she waved her hand.

"Wearing out your children is the best insomnia relief ever."

"I don't know if that's a good thing," he said.

"A good night of sleep is always a wonderful thing," she said, unable to count the number of sleepless nights she'd suffered during the past year.

"I guess so," he said and looked toward her. "As I said the other day, I really wasn't sure you would last more than a day or two. You just seemed so young."

"I'm small, but mighty," she joked.

"I'm starting to think that may be true. You've been full of surprises, though. Some secrets in your background. You put on a happy face, but I've seen a few moments of sadness in your eyes."

Nerves jangled in her stomach. She didn't know she'd given so much away. She thought she'd put on a good front. "You're very observant," she said. "I think most of us have experienced sadness by my age. I try not to dwell on it."

"Was it the loss of your parents?" he asked.

"That was painful, but there has been an avalanche of other issues and events that have been life-changing for my sister and brother since that time. Our future became uncertain," she said, her heart squeezing with the pain of worry over her sister and brother. She just wanted them to be safe, and if at all possible, happy.

Gavin squeezed her shoulder. "I wish you could see your eyes. They look stormy and a little afraid. You know you're safe here, don't you?"

Sara took a deep breath. He'd nailed her emotions, making her feel uncomfortably vulnerable. At the same time, his hand on her shoulder was so comforting and the expression on his face was an exquisite combination of kindness and male strength. It would be so easy to give in to that. Too easy.

The moment stretched between them, and Sara knew she should turn away. But Gavin was compelling and she'd been strong a long time. He lowered his head toward hers and pressed his mouth against hers. His lips felt warm and sensual. Sara felt a wicked forbidden heat rush through her. His hands slid up to cup her jaw and the touch exuded both comfort and seduction. She'd never experienced that combination before and she couldn't help wanting more. Leaning toward him, she opened her mouth and he deepened the kiss. A ripple of awareness hummed through her.

"Daddy?"

Sam's little-boy voice broke the spell and Sara pulled back, appalled by her susceptibility to Gavin. She needed to get herself straight. She needed to get herself under control. She stood because she couldn't figure what else to do.

"Hey, big guy, what's up?" Gavin asked as if he had just been doing lawn work instead of shaking her up from the inside out.

"Can I have some water?" he asked.

"Sure," Gavin said and rose.

"I'll get it," Sara said. "I'd like some water, too. I'm ready to go to bed."

"Sara," Gavin began.

"No. Really," she insisted. She darted for the kitchen and poured water for Sam and herself. She returned to the den and offered the cup to Sam. "Here you go, sweetie. Good night to both of you," she said without meeting Gavin's gaze. And then she rushed to her room and closed the door.

Taking several deep breaths, she stood in the room and covered her face. What was wrong with her? During the past ten years, Sara had never put her needs before her duties. Never. She couldn't mess things up for her siblings now. Chantaine had offered them a safe place. She couldn't jeopardize that for her sister or brother even if her brother was nowhere to be found, and her sister was doing God knew what with God knew who.

She made a quick trip to the bathroom, splashed water on her face and brushed her teeth, then returned to her bedroom where she changed into her nightgown. Climbing into bed, she forced her eyes closed and told her brain to shut down. Easier said than done. Why was she so drawn to Gavin? He was just a single dad doing the best he could. What about him affected her down to her very core?

The next several days, Sara managed to avoid meeting Gavin's direct gaze, although it was challenging. The weather took a turn for the worse and she tried several methods to keep the children entertained. Soon enough, everyone showed signs of cabin fever. Sam whined and Adelaide cried.

Out of desperation, she took to the piano. She banged out some hard modern pieces. The kids turned silent, or maybe she just couldn't hear them. Sara played three songs, then looked at Adelaide sitting in her infant seat and Sam standing beside the piano. Both just stared at her.

Many people seemed to forget that the piano was a percussion instrument. Hard to ignore.

Sam stepped toward her and pressed down a key.

"Try another," she said. "It won't bite."

He pressed down another key, then another and another.

"Want to learn a tune?" she asked.

"What tune?" he asked.

"'Chopsticks,'" she said, and she began to play.

Fifteen minutes later, Sam had learned his part.

Sara caught him playing the piano again during some free time. Unfortunately, the rain continued and even "Chopsticks" couldn't save them.

Desperate, Sara took the children outside in the rain. Warning them this would only last a short time, she headed straight for the mud puddles. Sam jumped up and down, splashing her and Adelaide. The baby shrieked in delight. Sara was just glad both kids seemed happy and entertained.

She had every intention of taking them inside and bathing them.

But Gavin came home early and drove past them on his way up the driveway to the cottage. "Uh-oh," she said.

Sam looked at her. "Are we in trouble?"

"Maybe," she said with a wince.

"Maybe he won't be mad," Sam said hopefully.

With the rain streaming down on them, she stared at him and smiled. "Maybe not. It's just rain and a little mud," she said. "I guess we better go back," she said. Sam nodded.

They walked back to the cottage where Gavin stood at the open front door with his hands crossed over his chest.

"Hi, Daddy," Sam said, darting toward his father. "We've been splashing in the puddles."

"I can see that," Gavin said, pulling his son up into his arms. He sent an inquiring glance toward Sara.

"We got very, very bored," she admitted.

Gavin gave a slow nod.

"I thought we could all get a bath after a little time outside," she said.

"I can play 'Chopsticks,'" Sam told Gavin.

"What?" Gavin asked Sam.

"I can play 'Chopsticks,'" Sam repeated. "Sara says I'm 'cellent."

Gavin smiled at his son. "I bet you are." He met Sara's gaze. "Let's get those baths."

Moments later, Sara bathed Adelaide. Afterward she strapped the little girl into her baby seat and then rinsed herself in the shower. She toweled dry and quickly dressed herself. She took the baby carrier to the den.

Two minutes later, Gavin and Sam, scrubbed clean, entered the room. "We should play 'Chopsticks,'" Sam said to Sara.

"Sounds good to me," she said. She sat on the left side of the piano bench. Sam joined her on the right side. "I'll play it through one time, okay?" she said.

She started and Sam joined in after the first time. They played it through twice and ended with a flair. Sara lifted her hand in a victory clap to Sam.

Sam spun around on the bench. "I'm a musician," he shouted.

Gavin beamed and gave a thumbs-up. "You bet you are."

"And you're not mad because we played in the puddles?" Sam asked.

Gavin's expression softened. "I'm not mad. You looked like you were having a good time," he said, his gaze locked with Sara's. She saw a combination of gratitude and something else she couldn't quite name, but it made her heart skip a beat.

Hours later after they'd had dinner and both children had been put to bed, Sara tried to get her cup of water and escape to her room as usual, but Gavin caught her in the hallway.

"You're not avoiding me, are you?" he asked.

Sara searched for an honest, but gentle response. "I'm not sure I would use the word *avoiding*."

Gavin lifted a brow in speculation. "What word or words would you use? *Running scared?*"

Sara stiffened her back. "That's a bit extreme. Even insulting."

"You haven't given me an alternative explanation. Did you hate kissing me so much?" he asked.

Her heart stopped at his words, at the expression on his face. "No. I didn't hate it," she said.

"Then why have you been avoiding me like the plague?" he demanded.

"Because I liked it," she confessed, irritated. "I liked our kiss. Way too much."

Chapter Four

Thank heavens Gavin was too stunned to respond, so Sara was able to escape to her bedroom. She counted backward from five hundred to battle her insomnia but was still too worked up to fall asleep. Sara didn't know when she finally drifted off, but dawn seemed to arrive far too soon.

Sara raced into nanny mode as soon as her alarm rang. There was no time for Gavin to question her.

"We're visiting Princess Bridget and her family today," Sara told Gavin. "She has an American husband who is apparently determined to populate their property with many different animals."

Gavin poured coffee into a travel cup. "Sounds like an interesting day," he said.

Sara smiled. "I'm sure it will be. Princess Bridget is a wonder. Her boys will inspire Sam. Plus she has a baby daughter. There should be plenty of havoc. You shall wish you hadn't missed it."

"If you say so," Gavin said.

"I do," she insisted. "Bet you won't encounter animals today."

"Trust me," he said. "I'll encounter animals today. They just won't be cute and furry or feathery."

An hour later, Sara packed the children into the car and drove to Princess Bridget's home. A security man casually waved her through since she was expected. Approaching the home, Sara noticed the festive holiday wreaths and lights and made a mental note to work on decorations for the cottage. Sara carried Adelaide up the steps with Sam sticking close by her side. He'd been even more quiet than usual. Sara knocked on the door.

A woman answered with a nod and a smile. "You must be Sara. I'm Ms. Shelton," she said. "Please come in. Her Highness is waiting for you."

"Unless Princess Bridget gives you different instructions, remember to address her first as Your Highness and then as ma'am, just like we practiced," Sara told Sam.

Sam nodded in response. Ms. Shelton led them into a lovely but comfortable-looking room with upholstered couches, chairs, a Christmas tree in the corner and an open toy box against one of the walls. Bridget was seated and appeared to be wiping something off the face of her squirming baby, who was a few months older than Adelaide.

"Your Highness, your visitors are here," Ms. Shelton said.

Bridget immediately turned and shot them a brilliant smile. "Ah, here you are. I'm so glad you came,

Sash—" She broke off and deliberately said, "*Sara.* And you must be Samuel," she said bending toward him.

Sam nodded. "Yes, Your Highness. Sam."

"Oh, let's not worry over those titles. You may call me Miss Bridget. My boys should be along any minute now to help the nanny give you a tour of the ranch. Do you like animals?"

Sam nodded again. "Yes, ma'am," he said in a quiet voice.

"What a lovely young man you are. I hope you'll survive my boys," she murmured under her breath. Barely two seconds passed before the sound of pounding footsteps filled the house. The twins scrambled into the room, shirts untucked, hair sticking out and there was, if Sara wasn't mistaken, a bit of chocolate on one of their cheeks.

Bridget made a tsking sound. "Boys, I can tell that Miss Janet didn't get a chance to check you before you came downstairs. You were supposed to clean up and you're not at all tidy."

"We were in a race," one of the boys said.

"We want to go outside," the other said.

"After you clean up a bit more. Move along now," Bridget said. "We have guests who are waiting." She bent down and gave them each a kiss, softening her directives.

"Apologies," Bridget said. "They're wonderful, but I fear what they're teaching little Mia, here. She watches every move they make. I thought we would all take a little stroll, so your little red-haired darling could get a peek at the animals, too. We can let the boys stay out a bit longer while we bring the girls back inside and have some tea and a chat. Does that sound good?"

Sara glanced at Sam. "What do you think, Sam?"

Sam nodded. "Yes, ma'am."

Sara smiled and squeezed his shoulder. "Good job," she said. He didn't immediately dart away. Maybe, just maybe, he was starting to accept her a bit.

The boys soon returned and introductions were made. Sara breathed a sigh of relief when she saw how friendly the twins, Tyler and Travis, were toward Sam. The nanny, Miss Janet, appeared completely at ease with the boys and the ranch.

Bridget, wearing a floral dress and sweater, allowed the nanny to take the lead. "Miss Janet grew up on a farm, so she's keen to take the boys on all kinds of outdoor adventures."

The group viewed the horses, goats and chickens, then Sara and Bridget and the babies returned to the house.

Bridget spread an activity blanket on the floor with some toys and Sara placed Adelaide on the blanket.

"So, how is your new temporary position working out?" Bridget asked as Miss Shelton brought a tray of tea and biscuits into the room.

"It has been an adventure," Sara said. "Because I had enjoyed leading volunteer music activities with children in most of the cities where I performed, I thought it would be an easy transition. I'm glad I received some training with your nanny and children. Especially since Sam and his father are still dealing with their grief. I will say this," she added, "With the exception of a few nights when my mind was too busy, I can't remember when I've slept this well."

Bridget gave a hearty laugh. "Good for you. I was a bit concerned when Ericka told me about this scheme, but you did very well with my children during your training. Plus you seem quite determined. How is your sister doing?"

Sara wrinkled her brow in concern. "My sister has a different personality than I do. She's more about living for the moment. I worry, but that's my nature. She seems to be doing fine. Thank you for asking."

"And you find Mr. Sinclair agreeable?" Bridget asked, sipping her tea.

"I can see that he's doing the best he can as a single dad," Sara said.

"I can relate. When I first met my husband, he was a single dad to the twins and working as a doctor at a hospital. You do have a relief nanny, don't you?" she asked.

Sara hesitated a bit too long.

Bridget shook her head. "Well, that is not acceptable at all. It's difficult enough for you to go from being a concert pianist and princess to a nanny. And, yes, I know it's temporary and for your own good. But everyone needs backup for child care. I had this same discussion with my sister Ericka less than a year ago. We need to do something about that right away."

"It may not be that easy," Bridget said, biting her lip. "The children aren't bad, but it's a challenging situation. Sam is upset. He's so quiet and he tenses up almost every time I touch his shoulder. Adelaide is teething quite a bit, which makes her miserable. This is a good day," she said, nodding toward the red-haired tot chewing on a toy. "By the end of the day, we put the children to bed and I go to bed right after that."

"Well, that explains why Mr. Sinclair hasn't accepted any invitations for dinner at the palace," Bridget said. "I'll figure something out. Don't worry."

"I'm not worried," Sara said. "We're doing much better than we were the first few days."

"Excellent," Bridget said, but Sara suspected that Bridget was making plans. "I know we're trying to keep your presence in Chantaine a secret, but I'm sure my sisters would love an opportunity to have you and your sister for tea at the palace." Bridget lifted her finger. "Before you say no, I'll make sure that the children have proper care."

"Thank you, but I don't want you to go to any extra trouble. I will ask a different favor, however. I'm concerned about celebrations for the Christmas holidays. Mr. Sinclair seems reluctant to decorate the cottage. He says he wants everything low-key and says all their decorations are in storage back in the States."

Bridget shot her a look of horror. "Well, you must decorate. The palace has tons of extra decorations. I'll make sure to have some delivered to the cottage."

"Thank you. I think it would be good for everyone. No matter what's going on in your life, Christmas decorations have a way of lifting your spirit."

"I so agree," Bridget said with a nod.

At that moment, there was a stampede of footsteps in the foyer. Bridget's twins raced into the room, breathless. "Sam is bleeding!" they both said at once.

Panic coursed through Sara and she raced toward the front door. "Bleeding," she repeated. She shouldn't have turned his care over to anyone. *She* was responsible. *She* should have kept him safe.

Running out the front door, she saw him coming up the steps with skinned knees and a scraped face. "Oh, Sam," she said and pulled him into her arms.

"I'm okay," he said. "I'm okay. I ran after the goats and fell down. I'm okay. I'm okay."

Miss Janet nodded. "He's a very brave boy."

"Of course he is," Sara said, her chest twisting with emotion. "Let's clean up your scrapes."

Sam nodded. "I'm okay."

Sara continued hugging him and for several seconds, he didn't pull away.

After she bandaged his wounds, they returned home and both children went down for a nap. Sara spent the next two hours recovering from her panic. She knew Sam would be fine, but what if something worse had happened? Even though she'd received a bit of emergency training, Sara wondered if she was truly prepared for that possibility.

After the children awakened from their naps, Sara served them an early dinner. Soon afterward, Gavin walked through the door.

Sara raced to meet him. "I need to warn you. Sam was hurt today."

Gavin blinked. "Is he in the hospital?"

"Oh, no," she said. "Band-Aids. Antibiotic ointment. He got scraped running after Princess Bridget's goats."

Gavin shrugged. "Was he upset?"

"Not remotely," she said. "He kept saying, I'm okay. I'm okay."

"Good for him," he said. "Where is he?"

"In the kitchen," she said.

Gavin went into the kitchen. "Hey, big guy, how was your day?"

"I chased goats," Sam said, proudly flashing the Band-Aid on his cheek.

"I hope this incident isn't the start of a trend," Sara said.

"Miss Sara almost cried," Sam said.

"Of course I did. I didn't want you to be hurt," she told him.

Sam rolled his eyes. Not even five years old, but he rolled his eyes.

"I think he's starting to like you," Gavin whispered.

"We'll see," she said, still skeptical. "Would you like some casserole? I can heat it up."

"What did you eat?" he asked.

"Nothing yet," she said.

"Casserole for both of us," he said and sat down at the table with his children.

She warmed up the casserole and they hurriedly consumed it while they entertained the kids. Gavin rinsed the dishes and put them in the dishwasher. Sara liked him for that. He bathed Sam. She bathed Adelaide and went to the kitchen to get her cup of water.

Gavin met her just before she escaped from the kitchen. He put his hands on her waist and steadied her. "Whoa. Caught you before you went to your room. Is my company that bad?"

Sara sighed. "No. I'm just trying to stay out of trouble."

Gavin's eyes darkened. "I'm innocent. Just look at me."

Sara shook her head. "Not for me."

He stared into her eyes. "Okay. What if we just sit on the porch and talk? I won't make any moves on you."

Sara felt a sliver of disappointment, but chastised herself for the feeling. "That sounds nice," she said.

Gavin poured two glasses of wine and led her outside to the porch.

Sara vowed to take only a few sips. Being with Gavin affected her far more than it should have.

Gavin took a seat and she followed. "Sounds like it was an interesting day," he said, swirling the wine in his glass.

"It was," she said, and she took a sip of the red wine. "Princess Bridget is much calmer than I recalled. I was so upset when Sam got hurt."

Gavin nodded. "Kids will terrify you." He paused. "You did well. If you're not feeling anything, then you're not living. Sam felt something today. He chased those goats. He felt some joy. That's rare for him."

Silence stretched between them. Sara thought about what Gavin had just said. He was right. Sam had been very short on joy most of the time.

"I want him to feel joy much more often," she said. "But I don't want him to end up in the hospital because of it."

Gavin laughed. "We can work on that."

"How?" she asked.

"I'm not sure," he said, taking a drink of wine. "But I think you made a breakthrough today."

"With a goat," she said.

He chuckled, and it was far too sexy to her. "They didn't have any cattle?"

"Two, but the goats were far more active."

"They presented more of a challenge. A boy needs a challenge," he said.

"Well, thank goodness he's going to preschool tomorrow," she said.

Another silence passed.

"Thanks for not quitting," he said.

"Quitting was never a consideration," she said.

"That fact makes you entirely too tempting to me," he said.

"Then I'll remove the temptation and go to bed," she said. She stood.

"Well, that's no fun," he said.

She swallowed her laughter at his comment. "I'm not here to be fun," she said. "Except at times for the children."

"Well, damn," he said.

Sara felt tempted, seduced, amused. Forcing herself to deny it, she pressed her lips together. "Trust me. This is best for everyone. Good night." She went to her bedroom, facing another night of counting backward from one thousand because five hundred wasn't working.

The next night, Gavin arrived home and made sure he wore out the kids. After he and Sara put them to bed, he made sure to block her before she made her way to the bedroom.

"There you are again," she said. She licked her too-sexy lips.

"Yeah. You're teaching me," he said. "You keep trying to disappear."

"I'm not disappearing," she said. "I'm just going to sleep."

"How long does it take you to go to sleep?" he asked.

Sara paused. "Well, Sam does have my sound machine."

"Good point. I've placed an order for one," Gavin said, sighing. "On a different subject, I've been asked repeatedly to attend a palace dinner, but I've dodged the invitation so far."

"You should go," she said, her eyes bright with encouragement.

"You've been invited to come with me," he said.

She lifted her eyebrows. "Oh, wow."

He met her gaze, seeing trepidation. He mentally swore, wishing he didn't feel like a teenager asking a girl out on a date.

"One of the princesses left a message saying she would send someone to watch over the kids," he said.

"Bridget," she muttered.

"Well, are you game?" he asked.

She sighed. "I'm not sure this is a good idea." She met his gaze for a long moment. "But you need to get out," she said. She took another breath. "So, I'll do it."

"Is that a pity response?" he asked.

"Of course not," she said, but he wasn't sure if he believed her.

"Hey, I can turn it down. I've done it before," he said. "I just figured if I go once, I won't have to go again."

"You shouldn't turn them down every time. They'll find it unfriendly," she said. "I'll go. *We* will go. But they'll probably ask you again. I hear the royal family enjoys visitors, especially Americans since several of them married Americans."

"You seem to know a lot about them," he said.

Sara gave a shrug and looked a bit discomfited. "Well, I did my apprenticeship with Princess Bridget. She's very outgoing and chatty."

"You have a very interesting background," he said.

She shrugged again. "It's not that interesting," she said. "If I hadn't had all those different nannies, my upbringing would have been pretty narrow."

He wasn't quite satisfied with Sara's response. Something about her didn't add up. All those nannies. Her family must have been loaded, and now she was the nanny for his kids?

"And your parents?" he prodded.

"From a different generation. A different era. Times have changed so quickly in the past fifty years. Technology, traditions. Don't you agree? Aren't your parents much different than you?"

"I guess so," he said, thinking of how his divorced parents had moved on with their lives and not wanted to bother with him and the kids after his wife had died. "My dad is busy golfing. My mother is busy playing bridge and traveling, but surprisingly enough, she's not interested in coming to visit us in Chantaine. I think we're a little too sad for her. Lauren's mother died several years ago, and she was never close with her father."

"That's unfortunate," she said. "Your mother is missing out. Even when he's sad, Sam is a wonder. And Adelaide," she said, chuckling. "She would rock everyone's world. On the other hand, your mother may have her own pain and perhaps she just can't see past it."

"Insightful," he said. "That's giving her the benefit of the doubt."

"I find life is much easier when you give people the benefit of the doubt."

"Where'd you learn that?"

She lifted an eyebrow and shot him a grin. "From one of my many nannies, of course. And now, I'm going to bed."

"Will you sleep?" he asked as she turned away from him.

"At some point. Good night," she said and walked away from him, her posture perfectly erect.

Gavin stared after her. She was such a contradiction. Scrubbed clean face, casual clothes, but oh-so proper manners and a restrained attitude. Who was she?

He was much more curious than he should be. At the same time, when he was around her, he felt…more. He'd been dead for what seemed like ages. Far before his wife died. After she passed away, he'd been desperate to bring himself, Sam and Adelaide back to life, and Chantaine had seemed the perfect place. It had turned out much more complicated than he'd expected.

Sam was inching forward, though. Yesterday was a breakthrough even though it had involved scrapes and bandages. Adelaide was far more calm under Sara's influence. Sara just seemed to spin some sort of magic over all of them. Even him. Even his sad, cynical self, although he still ran from terrible moments of guilt. He still wondered what he could have done to make things turn out differently for his wife and no wave machine would help him sleep through that.

The following night, Gavin came home dragging, but Sara noticed that he seemed determined to help with the kids. "Let's do an outside adventure," he said.

"Yeah," Sam agreed. "Outside. Do we have to take Adelaide?"

Gavin laughed. "Adelaide is your baby, too. We need to take care of her."

"But all she does is sit and scoot," Sam said. "And cry and poop."

"That's what you did at her age," Gavin said.

"I can keep Adelaide while you two go outside," Sara said.

"No. I'm taking both my kids outside tonight."

"I already took them outside," she said. "But I'm sure they would enjoy being out there with you."

Gavin paused. "You want to come with us?" he asked.

She couldn't resist his request. "I would love that."

After a quick diaper change for Adelaide, Sara put the baby in the stroller and urged Sam to take a quick potty break. Moments later, they began their adventure.

"I see something pink," Gavin said.

"A flower," Sam said, pointing at a blooming anemone.

"Good," Gavin said. "What do you see, Sara?"

"I see something gray," she said, pushing the stroller alongside Sam and Gavin.

"The road," Sam said. "The road is gray."

"Good job," Gavin said. "Your turn, Sam. What do you see?"

Sam looked up. "I see something white and fluffy."

Gavin glanced at Sara and shared a smile with her. "What's white and fluffy?"

"The clouds in the sky. I see something green…"

And so it went for the next fifteen minutes. By the time they arrived back at the house, Gavin appeared refreshed and Sam was more relaxed. Adelaide was hungry. She wailed until she was fed, then banged on her tray and spit out her excess food.

Somehow, minutes turned to hours during feeding and bathing and bottles and reading books. Sara washed dishes while Gavin put both children to bed. Just as she was sudsing a frying pan, she felt warmth behind her and a hand join hers in the sink.

"Need some help?" he asked, sliding his hand through hers in the soapy water.

Sara's heart tripped over itself at the sensation. Dishwater. A man's hand over hers. Why should that affect her?

"I'm almost finished," she said, but for just a few

extra seconds, she savored the sensation of his fingers laced through hers in the warm water.

She drained the sink and rinsed the last dish, hyperaware of the fact that Gavin stood behind her, his strong body warming the back of hers. He felt so solid, so male. She couldn't help leaning back against him—just for a quick moment, she told herself.

Out of her peripheral vision, she noticed Gavin grabbing a dish towel to dry his hands. Then he slid his hands across the front of her waist. "You feel so good, Sara."

He guided her to turn toward him and he lowered his mouth to hers for a long, soulful kiss. "I didn't know I'd ever feel this way again. I want you," he told her.

Chapter Five

Sara couldn't breathe. A dozen emotions roiled through her. Want, need, denial... She closed her eyes, trying to gain control. Shaking her head, she squeezed his hands. "This isn't a good idea. I shouldn't. You shouldn't..."

"Maybe," he said. "Maybe not."

"I'm your employee," she said, trying to stay firm even though it was all she could do not to lean into him. "I'm caring for your children. My focus needs to be on your children. Not on you. Not on how I feel about—"

"About me?" he asked.

She felt as if she were sinking into his chocolate-brown gaze. Quicksand. She felt as if she were walking in it. She closed her eyes again. "Mr. Sinclair," she began.

"I'm not Mr. to you," he said. "I'm Gavin."

Her heart slamming in her chest, she pressed her lips together and licked them.

"You know I'm right," he said.

Her stomach twisted. "This is so complicated. I don't want to mess up things with your children."

Sara felt Gavin take a deep breath and then exhale. "I get it," he said. "I don't want to mess things up for my kids either. I didn't expect to feel this way."

"Neither did I," she said. "It's probably just the proximity."

"I don't know." He gave a rough chuckle. "I haven't had this problem with the other nannies."

The way he looked at her made her heart jump. *She had to resist.* "Would it be better if I left? If you got a different nanny—"

"Hell, no," he said. "The kids are getting used to you. I'm not a rabid animal. I can restrain myself. If you can," he added with a hint of challenge in his eyes.

"Of course," she said. *Of course I can control myself.* She always had. It wouldn't be any different this time.

The following day, Sara took Sam to preschool and arrived back home to a large number of boxes on the front porch of the cottage. Carrying Adelaide to the pile, she spotted an envelope with her and Gavin's name on it. She opened it and found a note from Bridget. "A tree and a few holiday trinkets from the palace to make your season merry. All the best, Bridget."

Sara glanced at Adelaide. "Well, I guess I know what I'll be doing today."

Taking Adelaide inside the cottage, she strapped the baby into the infant seat and prayed she would get five to ten minutes to get the boxes inside before Adelaide began to squawk. Adelaide actually gave her more time because she seemed fascinated by Sara rushing in and out the front door.

Sara opened a few of the boxes and laughed at the combination of decorations. An artificial white Christmas tree. "Probably because Chantaine hasn't seen snow in a century," she said to Adelaide. She pulled out a wreath with bells, a musical snow globe and ornaments galore. There was even a toy train set.

Just as Adelaide began to squirm and make impatient sounds, Sara put her on her tummy on a play blanket and hoped the baby wouldn't be acquiring more scooting skills until after the holiday season because there was plenty the tot could get into.

The rest of the morning, Sara alternated between entertaining Adelaide and unpacking boxes. Before she knew it, it was time to pick up Sam from preschool. Bursting with hope and anticipation, she restrained herself. Sam was not at all interested in discussing his time at preschool, so she didn't force it and put on the radio to keep from blabbing about the Christmas decorations.

When she strode up the porch and flung open the door, she held her breath as she waited for Sam's excitement. What Sara hoped more than anything was that the Christmas decorations would lift his spirit. She wanted the whole family to feel the joy.

Sam stopped and stared silently at the tree, the train and the boxes. He looked up at her. "The tree should be green," he said and walked down the hallway to his room.

Sara's heart sank. She'd been so hopeful. She shook her head at herself. How could a few decorations cause the healing of such a deep wound? She looked at the fake white tree and wondered if she should take it down.

She wondered if she should remove all the decorations. Gavin had expressed his disinterest in making a big to-do over the holidays. Maybe she should have listened to him.

Sara took a deep breath and closed her eyes. Maybe she shouldn't make a snap decision. Why not wait until tomorrow? The only thing she had to lose was Gavin's scorn. Perhaps both of the Sinclair men would change their minds sooner rather than later.

Sam left his room when she called him for lunch. He was so quiet, the only thing she could hear was his chewing and crunching. As soon as he finished, she engaged him in a dice game in an effort to draw him out.

"Can I watch TV?" he asked.

"May I please," she corrected.

"Yes," he said with a nod.

"Repeat it," she said, biting back a smile.

Sam looked put-upon. "May I please watch TV?"

"After a thirty minute rest," she said. She'd learned to avoid the word *nap* because Sam was convinced he was far too old for naps.

"Okay," he said grudgingly.

Sara put down Adelaide and took advantage of the quiet time by slumping on the sofa and closing her eyes. Funny how the attitude toward naps changed as one grew up a little bit. Shortly, she felt a tug on her arm and glanced up to see Sam looking at her.

"Is rest time over?"

Sara glanced at her watch in surprise. "Why, yes it is. Right on the dot. You may watch an hour of television. Then we'll take a walk when Adelaide wakes up."

Sara noticed that Sam seemed to completely ignore the Christmas tree. He didn't exhibit the tiniest bit of curiosity even in the toy train set. Discouraged, she took care of tasks around the house until Adelaide awakened and she took the children for a walk. She played racing games with Sam to keep it interesting.

"Run to the corner and back. See if you can make it back before Adelaide and I arrive at the corner," she challenged.

Sam pumped his short legs and she could almost see a hint of a smile. On his return run, a man carrying a ladder walked out of a driveway and Sara saw a potential collision. Panic rushed through her.

"Sam! Watch out!" she yelled, rushing toward him as she pushed the stroller.

"Hey, there," the man said, dropping the ladder and catching Sam before he hit the ground.

Her heart pounding, she reached for Sam. "Are you okay?"

He allowed her to touch his shoulders and nodded.

She sighed in relief. "Thank you for catching him. We were playing a game of running. Trying to work off some energy. Maybe I'd better try a different game plan next time."

The man nodded. "Everybody's fine," he said, extending his hand. "I'm Michael Trevon. I own this house, but a renter lives here, so I was taking care of some repairs. So, these two are yours?"

She nodded. "Yes," she said. "Well, in a way," she added and smiled. "I'm their nanny."

"I suspect they keep you busy," he said.

"They do indeed," she said, finally looking at the man's face. He had kind eyes with wrinkles at the corners, light hair covered by a cap. An American look, she thought, but she heard a wisp of a German accent.

it down tomorrow afternoon," she said. Then she wandered into the living room to say good-night to Sam.

The boy was standing in front of the tree staring at it. He shook his head. "Maybe more ornaments will help it," he said.

Surprise rushed through her and she gazed at Gavin. His lips twitched. "Looks like we're going to have a white Christmas tree this year, after all."

Gavin put Sam to bed and kissed his son's forehead. He headed toward his bedroom. He and Sam had played a video game and Sam had hung ten ornaments on the crazy white Christmas tree. The plan was to do more decorating tomorrow.

Gavin felt ambivalent about the whole issue. He wasn't sure all this decorating would turn out well. At the same time, Sam had exhibited interest, so Gavin would encourage his interest. He took a long breath and thought about going back to the den, but he wasn't in the mood.

Returning down the hall, he heard sounds from Sara's room. He stood outside her door. Muffled sounds of distress issued from her room.

Concerned, Gavin went into her room. She thrashed from side to side in her bed, moaning. "Alex," she said. "I can't breathe. I can't breathe. Alex. Tab…"

Her distress stabbed at him. He sat on the edge of her bed and gently squeezed her shoulders. "Sara," he said quietly.

"Alex—"

"Sara," he said a bit louder.

She paused, shaking her head and breathing heavily. "Help," she said.

"You look a bit familiar," he said. "I can't put my finger on it, but I feel like I've seen you before. Ever been to Berlin?"

"A couple times," she said, wondering if he'd possibly attended one of her concerts or seen her photograph in a newspaper. "I think I just have one of those everywoman faces."

"I wouldn't say every woman is a beauty like you," he said.

She blinked at the comment. "You're too kind. Thank you again for saving Sam from a spill. We really should get back home," she said as she turned around. "Come along, Sam."

"I didn't catch your name," he said.

"Sara," she said over her shoulder.

"Well, if you need assistance, Sara, let me know. I'm up here frequently looking after my property."

"Thank you," she said. "Have a good day."

She told herself not to be spooked by the exchange, but she was. Even though Chantaine was a charming island with wonderful people, no one could escape the reality that they were living in an internationally accessible world. She'd been on enough public stages that someone she came across might recognize her, and that wouldn't do at all.

A couple hours later, as Sara heated soup that the part-time cook had prepared, Gavin arrived from work. She heard him stop and imagined his thoughts as he looked at the tree, the train and boxes of decorations.

He walked into the kitchen. "Soup smells good," he said.

"You hired a good cook," she said and forced a smile.

"The decorations are interesting," he said.

"The palace sent them," she said, stirring the soup.

"The tree is white," he said as if he couldn't grasp it.

"They don't get snow here, so it's meant to look like snow," she said.

"Oh," he said. "Where's Sam?"

"Hiding out in his bedroom. I don't think he was happy with the decorations," she said.

"I told you I thought we shouldn't overdo the holidays," he said.

"I know," she said. "I'll take them down tomorrow if they still bother you. I was just hoping—"

"What? That Christmas decorations would miraculously transform his mood, lift his depression and turn him into a smiling child? Didn't anyone ever tell you that Santa Claus isn't real? Christmas can't fix everything, even though even I wish it could."

"I'm not suggesting that it can, but if there's a chance to infuse this difficult time with a little joy, I don't see what's wrong with it." She paused for half a beat. "And if you'll pardon my saying so, you sound extremely cynical."

He narrowed his eyes. "Well, if you'll pardon my saying so, the past few years of my family's life hasn't exactly been magical or a fairy tale. And my marriage—" He broke off. "Just forget I said that. Sam and I have an appointment with the therapist tonight. We need to eat as soon as possible so we can leave on time."

Dinner was quiet and stilted, but blessedly swift. As soon as Gavin and Sam left, Sara's fingers itched to decorate the tree, but she restrained herself. She would only be making more work for herself if the two Sinclair men decided they wanted the decorations taken down.

Instead, she entertained Adelaide and took out some of her frustration on the piano in the den. Playing the piano was one area where she felt a modicum of success. As she played, she couldn't help thinking about the fact that she hadn't heard anything from her brother in nearly a year. She didn't know if he was alive or dead. Add to that the limbo that she and her sister had remained in for the past year, and Sara realized the decorations were as much for herself as they were for the Sinclairs.

She was grateful that the royal Devereaux family of Chantaine had provided asylum for her sister and herself, but she was growing impatient with the ongoing sense of being in a waiting room.

Pushing back her feelings took more effort than usual. She was beginning to understand her sister Tabitha's unwillingness to put her entire life on hold. Sara read a book to Adelaide and put the baby down.

No sooner had she fixed herself a cup of tea than Sam and Gavin came into the house. She met Gavin's gaze. "You're back a bit early. No stops along the way?"

He shook his head. "Promised a video game instead," he said.

His eyes looked dark like a storm ready to roll in. She'd already challenged him enough tonight. She wouldn't do it again. "All right, then. If you are putting Sam to bed, then I'll go read in my bedroom."

"You don't have to sequester yourself," he said.

"It's okay. It's a quiet, calming time of day for me. Good night, then," she said and got her cup of water.

"Your intentions were good," Gavin said. "We're just not in a good place for Christmas this year."

"I understand. I'm sorry if I forced it on you. I'll take

"Sara," he said again.

Her eyes fluttered and she looked up at him, clearly not recognizing him for several seconds. Then she took a breath and met his gaze. "Gavin," she whispered.

He nodded, relieved that she was awake and somewhat cognizant. "I think you were having a nightmare."

"The fire," she said, and she reached for his hands. "The fire. It was terrible. I could barely breathe. I couldn't find Alex or Tabitha. I was so afraid. Crawling on the floor."

Gavin squeezed her hands. "It was just a dream," he said.

Sara shook her head. "No. It really happened. A long time ago." She lifted her left hand. "I burned my fingertips. No fingerprints left on this hand. I couldn't play piano for a long time until I recovered."

Gavin looked at her left hand and saw the absence of fingerprints. He wondered what kind of hell she had gone through. "Did you suffer any other injuries?"

"Just smoke inhalation," she said. "Alex tried to come for me, but they wouldn't let him. He wasn't sure how long he could safely wait before coming back inside."

There was a lot to this story that he wasn't hearing right now, but Gavin knew he needed to help Sara calm down. She needed that more than questions. "You're safe now. There's no fire here," he told her. "We have smoke alarms. I had them installed."

She took several breaths, then sighed. "I'm sorry if I disturbed you," she said. "I haven't had nightmares in a while."

He couldn't help wondering how long "a while" was. Instead of asking more questions, he nodded. "Get some rest. Do you need more water?" he asked, offering her some water.

Sara propped herself up on her elbows and took several sips of water. "That was good. I just need to settle down now."

"Is there anything I can do?" he asked.

She paused a half beat, then shook her head. "No, but thank you for waking me up before I became a screaming banshee."

He smiled. "You were nowhere near banshee level. Trust me, I know. Adelaide is my daughter."

Sara chuckled and seemed to relax. She took another deep breath. "I'll be okay now."

"Think about Santa Claus and reindeer," he said.

"And crazy white trees?"

"You might want to skip that one," he said.

She nodded and snuggled down into the covers. "It's not that bad. In my world, it would have been considered 'festive.'"

"Festive," he repeated. "I'll remember that. Close your eyes and imagine the ocean sound from the device we should be receiving any day. Damn international post."

Sara closed her eyes. "Crashing waves."

Gavin made a whooshing sound.

Sara smiled. "Nice try, but that sounds like the toilet."

Gavin smothered a laugh. "Okay, you make the sound."

Sara made a softer graduated whooshing sound.

"Yeah," he said. "Yours was better."

She made the sound again.

"Okay, stop now and go to sleep," he said, looking

down at her. It was all he could do not to kiss her. Her forehead, her cheek, her lips. Gavin gritted his teeth. There were so many ways he could make her forget about that bad dream.

"Thank you," she whispered, her eyes still closed.

"No problem," he said. Then he rose and went to bed. But he sure didn't go to sleep. Who was Alex? Who was Tabitha? What was Sara's history? She was more complicated than she pretended. He wondered what else he didn't know about her. Plenty, he suspected. Plenty.

Gavin closed his eyes, but his mind was flying in different directions. Who was she? She seemed so sweet. Where was she from? She was tender and complicated. With her face scrubbed clean, she looked like an innocent teenager, but he knew there was far more to her and her past.

Gavin closed his eyes again, but sleep was far, far away. Giving up, he rose from his bed and turned on his laptop. He might as well get some work done.

Sara awakened to the sound of Adelaide singing. *No, screaming.* She raced into the nursery and cooed and comforted the baby. "Rough wake-up, sweetie pie." She gathered the baby against her.

Adelaide immediately quieted.

"Oh, poor baby," she murmured. "It's hard being a baby, isn't it?"

Adelaide gave a squeaky sound.

Sara stroked the baby's head. "I bet a bottle will help."

Sara walked to the kitchen and fixed a bottle for the baby. Adelaide sucked it down, then burped loudly and shot her a milky smile.

Sara blinked at the strong smell of formula and nodded. "So you feel better now?"

She placed her into her infant seat as Gavin strode into the kitchen wearing his pajamas. His hair mussed, he scrubbed his face with his hand. "I couldn't believe it when my alarm when off. Where did the night go?" he muttered.

"Sometimes they seem to pass in seconds," she said. After a pause, she added, "I'm sorry about my nightmare."

"I'm sure it was worse for you than me. It looked like a rough dream to me," he said, heading for the coffeemaker.

Sara took a deep breath. "I thought I had buried the memory."

"I'm not sure that's the kind of memory that can be buried. Some of those kinds of memories have to be worked out more than once. They leave scars, but they can make you stronger, too," he said.

"Maybe," she said.

He nodded. "Sometimes you have to think about it even if you don't want to. So the shrink says."

"Is that how you handle your late wife's death?" she asked.

Gavin's face turned to stone, and she knew she shouldn't have mentioned his wife. It was clearly a taboo subject for him.

He shook his head. "There's no good way to handle her death. I hate that she died. I hate it for the kids. I hate it for her. I blame myself. Our marriage wasn't what it should have been for the last couple of years. I tried, but I couldn't—" He broke off and shook his head. "That's more than you wanted to know. I just wanted to tell you that you can turn that horrible experience into something good. I'll drink some coffee and take a shower," he said as he turned away.

Sara looked after him, wishing she could comfort him, wishing she hadn't mentioned his late wife. Why had she?

Obviously, all had not been well between Gavin and his wife. Many people tried to pin the blame on one of the spouses, but even Sara had learned that it took two to make a relationship work and there were many things that could make it break down.

She'd glimpsed pain in Gavin's eyes when he talked about his late wife. She wondered if he would ever be able to heal.

Chapter Six

Life in the household muddled on. Sara and Sam decorated the tree and shortly afterward, Sam became fascinated by the toy train beneath it. Mid-December brought extra rain to the island of Chantaine and Sara struggled to find ways to entertain the children during the wet times. She resorted to playing the piano on the darkest days.

Halfway through a piece by Beethoven, she heard a knock at the door and went to answer it. Mr. Trevon, the neighbor, appeared wearing a smile and holding a package.

"Hi there. The post delivered this to my door, but I believe it was intended for you. I remembered your name was Sara," he said, holding out the package.

"Thank you very much," she said. "I guess everyone makes mistakes."

Mr. Trevon shrugged. "Guess so. Was that you playing the piano? If so, you are concert-worthy," he said.

Sara demurred. "You flatter me. I'm no Mozart. But I love to play," she said.

He narrowed his eyes. "You look like someone I've seen before. And I'd swear there's some connection to music, but I just can't put my finger on where I would have seen you. Are you sure you're not a professional?"

Sara bit the inside of her lip. She hated to be untruthful. "You sound like a music lover yourself. I, too, love music, but professional? I aspire. There are so many others who are more talented and accomplished than I am. As a music lover, I'm sure you understand."

Mr. Trevon nodded, but he still looked at her curiously. "Of course, I understand."

"Thank you again," she said.

"Good day," he said.

Her heart racing, Sara stared after him as he walked away. It wouldn't do for him to figure out her real identity. It wouldn't do at all.

She felt a tug at her pants leg and looked down at Sam.

"What's in the package?" he asked.

"Well, let's find out." She went to the kitchen to get some scissors. Delving through the wrapping, she pulled out the sleep sound machine and smiled. Gavin hadn't been joking when he'd said he'd ordered it for her. She put the enclosed batteries into it and pushed the button for the sound of ocean waves. "Does this sound familiar?" she asked.

Sam nodded, his curiosity satisfied. "Can I play a video game?"

"Thirty minutes," she said. She listened to the waves

for a moment longer, but the sound didn't calm her like it usually did. What if the neighbor had seen her in concert or perhaps seen her photo in a newspaper? Sara's stomach tightened. How much longer was she going to be able to hide who she truly was?

The following night, Sara dressed for dinner at the palace with Gavin. She'd actually been preparing bit by bit most of the afternoon. She told herself not to be excited, but this was the first time she'd dressed up in ages, and she could barely remember the last time she'd been out on a date. Even though this wasn't really a date, she reminded herself for the fiftieth time.

"So, stop being excited," she sternly instructed herself as she applied her makeup.

Although Sara traveled light these days, she always packed a little black dress. As she dressed for the event, she tamped down her feelings of excitement. Sam alternately joined her and his father in different bathrooms.

Sam stared up at her. "Dad doesn't use a pencil on his eyes."

"I'm sure he doesn't, but I bet he shaves his face," she said, applying eye shadow.

"Yeah, but he doesn't put stuff on his eyes," he said.

"It's customary for women to put on makeup for an evening out," she said.

Sam watched her as she applied mascara. "I'm glad I'm not a girl," he said. "I don't want to put that stuff on my eyes."

"Eyelashes," she corrected. "Women have to be tough. Never forget that."

He nodded solemnly. "Who is going to take care of Adelaide tonight?"

Her heart immediately softened. Sam was a little

afraid and he was putting it onto Adelaide. Sara turned away from the mirror.

"Princess Bridget has arranged for a wonderful caretaker tonight. Her name is Binnie. You may need to help Adelaide adjust to her," she said, Lifting him from where he stood on the commode to the floor. "Do you think you can do that?"

Sam nodded slowly. "Yes, I will."

Her heart caught at the sad expression on his face. "You can call your father at any time. You'll probably like Binnie. She probably won't make you listen to the piano," she teased.

"I kinda like the piano," he said.

"Thank you." She reached down to kiss him on the cheek. He froze for a half second, but didn't pull away.

A tiny step forward, Sara thought, catching her breath.

Sara heard a knock at the door. "I bet that's Binnie. We should greet her."

"I'll go." Sam barreled down the hallway.

It was time to go. Sara felt a flutter of nerves then rolled her eyes at herself. After one last glance in the mirror, she grabbed her shawl and strode down the hall.

She stepped into the den and Gavin turned to look at her. He blinked. "Wow."

Sara couldn't remember feeling more complimented. She tried to hide her pleasure, but she suspected she wasn't successful. She smiled. "Thank you."

Gavin, wearing a dark suit, white shirt and red tie, looked pretty amazing himself. His eyes glittered with something sexy and forbidden. Something she shouldn't be thinking about. Something too seductive.

"Are you ready?" he asked.

Not really, she thought. "Yes," she said, and she accepted his arm.

Gavin escorted her to the car. During the drive, she felt aware of his presence. She'd known he was tall and had a muscular body, but she'd tried to ignore that fact. Now, as he drove toward the palace, she couldn't.

Gavin pulled to a stop at an intersection and adjusted his tie. "I'm not sure this is my scene. A palace?"

"Think of it as an historical hotel that probably needs major refurbishment," she said, remembering the state of the so-called palace in which she had lived.

"Major refurbishment?" he echoed. "That bad? How do you know this?"

Sara bit her lip. "It's just an educated guess. I've visited several palaces that needed quite a bit of work. Think about it. Palaces are like museums. They require a lot of upkeep."

"Hmm," he said. "I guess you're right. Still don't understand how you know so much about this."

"It was one of my courses at University. Historical preservation," she said, fudging the origin of her knowledge.

Silence followed. "You look beautiful tonight," he said.

Her heart tripped a beat. "Thank you. I made an effort. Not like every day."

"You're beautiful every day," he said. "But you knocked me off balance tonight."

Sara bit her lip again. "Amazing what a little mascara, lipstick and some heels can do."

"It's more than that," he said. "I think you may make a habit of hiding your beauty."

"You flatter me," she said.

"No," he said. "Not really."

She had no answer for that. She glanced out her window at the stars. "Beautiful night, isn't it?" she said. "The stars are so bright."

"Yeah," he said and slid a sideways glance at her. "Beautiful in a lot of ways."

Sara leaned back against her seat and decided to be quiet. An uncomfortable silence was better than stoking the heat and want that Gavin was subtly exhibiting and that she was feeling in response.

Several moments later, they arrived at the palace and were waved past the guard. Gavin parked, then assisted her from the passenger seat. "Ready?" he asked.

"Yes, thank you," she said, accepting his arm. She tried to remember the last time an attractive man had escorted her to a formal event, but no man came to mind. Was her memory failing her? Or had Gavin grabbed hold of her attention?

She inhaled a breath to clear her mind, but instead she caught a whiff of his subtle cologne mixed with his masculine scent. The scent made her feel a little dizzy, but she couldn't resist the urge to inhale again.

He led her into the palace where aides directed them down the hallway to a ballroom. "They've done a good job maintaining the palace. It's an expensive process," she mused.

"How do you know that?" Gavin asked.

Sara's stomach clenched and she struggled to cover for her comment. "I mentioned it earlier. I took a class in historical preservation," she said. "It must cost a lot of money to make necessary repairs and renovations, don't you think? And this palace has been around for centuries."

"Good point," he said. "Hate to think of the plumbing upgrades," he said.

She smiled. "Exactly."

He squeezed her elbow as they entered the ballroom. "Lovely," she said, looking at the chandeliers and Christmas decorations.

"Gaudy," he said.

She looked at him and laughed. "Versailles is gaudy," she said. "This is elegant."

"If you say so," he said. "But I'm from Texas and North Dakota."

"Enjoy your night of grandeur," she said.

"I will," he said, meeting her gaze with a sensual darkening from his eyes.

Her heart tripped over itself. She was far too susceptible to him. Sara looked away. "Oh, look, there's Princess Bridget. And Princess Ericka."

"You seem to be familiar with them," he said.

"They've been generous to me," she said. "Remember, Princess Bridget's nanny was my teacher while I was an apprentice."

"She did a good job," he said.

She smiled up at him. "Thank you."

They took their seats at an assigned table and were served exquisite food. Between courses, Sara excused herself and visited Princess Ericka's table. She bent her knees in a quick curtsey. "Your Highness," she said.

Princess Ericka waved the formality aside. "No need. I would have to return it," she said. "How can I help you?"

"Thank you," Sara said. "I can't stop thinking about my brother, Alex. Have you heard anything?"

"I haven't," Ericka said with a sad expression.

"It's been a year," Sara said. "I don't know how much longer I can bear this. I know you understand. Can you imagine if Stefan or your youngest brother were missing for over a year?"

Ericka gave a slight wince. "I hear you. I will press Stefan."

"I'm willing to hire a private investigation service. I must know if he's alive and well," she said.

"Give me a few days," Ericka said. "I promise to get in touch with you."

"Thank you," Sara said. "I'm having nightmares when I sleep."

Ericka frowned in sympathy. "I'll do my best."

Sara nodded and returned to her seat beside Gavin.

"Anything you want to tell me?" he asked.

She shrugged. "I'm fine.

"That's a lie. Maybe you'll trust me someday," he said.

Filled with conflict, she turned toward him. "This isn't about you. It's all about me. Please forgive me."

"I want to help you," he said.

She smiled. "I will ask you when I can. In the meantime, I've been instructed to wait a while longer."

"May I ask what this concerns?" he asked.

She paused and waffled for a moment. "My brother. He's missing. That's all I can say. Please keep it confidential."

"I will." He took her hand in his. "You can trust me. But I can see that I'll have to earn that trust."

Her heart clenched in her chest. "Thank you." That was all she could say. She feared she'd already revealed too much. She could barely eat another bite. Her stomach shut down at the sight of the chocolate mousse dessert.

Everyone toasted the royal family then walked from the ballroom and out of the palace. “It was beautiful, wasn’t it?” she asked Gavin.

“It was nice. The food was good,” Gavin said.

Sara couldn’t help laughing. “All about the food for you?”

He shrugged. “What’s more important? The fillet was great.”

“Glad you enjoyed it,” she said as he led her to the car and assisted her into the passenger seat.

Gavin slid into the driver’s seat beside her. “Can’t figure you out. One minute you’re soup and sandwiches. The next, you’re all about atmosphere and chandeliers.”

She shot him a sly smile. “I’m versatile.”

He smiled back at her. “So you say.”

He put the car in gear and they drove away from the palace. They drove a few miles farther and Gavin pulled into a parking lot for a public beach. He glanced at her. “Okay? We can pretend we’re on a date and walk on the beach. We won’t be able to do that tomorrow night.”

She paused, thinking this was a big no-no, but pushed her reluctance aside. “Let’s go,” she said and grabbed his hand.

A moment later, he helped her from the car. Sara ditched her shoes and relished the sensation of sand between her toes.

“You’re still wearing your shoes,” she said.

“Somebody has to,” he said and led her toward the ocean.

“What if you get your shoes wet?”

“They won’t melt,” Gavin said. “I can buy more. I have more in my closet.”

She stumbled after him. "You're looser than I thought."

He glanced at her. "You thought I was a stick in the mud?"

She shrugged. "Well..." she said.

He pulled her against him and lowered his mouth to hers. She sank into him. He felt so good, so strong. He slid his tongue over her lips and she felt her knees weaken.

"You taste so good," he murmured into her mouth.

She clutched his shoulders. "Gavin," she whispered.

He slid his hands down over her shoulders to the sides of her breasts and lower.

Sara clung to him. His strength and sensuality emanated through her. She slid her fingers through his hair. The sound of the ocean waves flowed over her as he held her. She couldn't remember such an amazing experience.

Gavin pulled her even closer against him. "I want you," he muttered against her mouth. The sound vibrated throughout her body.

She wanted him, too. But should she have him? His desire echoed throughout her body. She clung to him and kissed him. A kiss that went on and on. She couldn't remember wanting anything, anyone this much.

"This is crazy," she whispered.

"Or crazy right," he said.

Maybe, she thought. *Maybe not.* "Why does this feel so right?" she asked. "Why do you feel so right?"

"I don't know," he said. "I would never have guessed that at a time like this something could be so right."

What is so right? she wondered. She took a deep breath and tried to clear her mind, but she still felt muddy. "How—" She shook her head.

"Not sure," he said, sliding his hand through a strand of her hair. "But we'll figure it out."

Sara wasn't sure how anything between them could work out. At the same time, she didn't want to move away from his warmth and passion.

She took a deep breath and still felt dizzy. "What now?"

"Gelato," he said.

She smiled. "They may not be open."

"Gotta try," he said, and he kissed her again, making her think about everything except gelato.

He led her toward the car. "C'mon. Let's get you some hazelnut."

Gavin drove at the speed of wind. Surprisingly enough, the gelato shop was still open. He ordered raspberry. She ordered hazelnut.

Since the temperature was warm, they sat outside the shop while they devoured the creamy confection. "Will you give me a bite?" he asked her.

She met his gaze. "Must I?

He laughed. "I guess not," he said.

She lifted a spoonful to him. "Here," she said.

He took a bite and nodded. "Good, but I like mine better."

"Are you going to give me a taste?" she asked.

He shot her a devilish grin. "Of course I will," he said as he offered her a taste.

Sara savored the flavor on her tongue. "Okay, I have to admit that's pretty good."

"Better than hazelnut?"

"Close," she said. "Very close."

"I can make it better than hazelnut," he told her, leaning toward her and brushing her lips with his.

"That's what I'm afraid of," she said. "I need to resist you, but you're making it very difficult." Sara closed her eyes and tried to rein in her feelings, but she hadn't felt this light and giddy in forever. This was all temporary and crazy, she told herself. She had no business getting involved with Gavin.

Taking a deep breath, she pulled back and glanced at her watch. "We should be getting back. The sitter will be expecting us. If the children didn't go down easily, they may be expecting us, too."

The light faded from his eyes. He gave a slow nod. "You made me forget for a few moments."

Her heart squeezed tight. "It's all a juggling act, don't you think?" she asked.

"Yes," he said. "Perfect description."

During the drive home, they talked very little. The silence felt deafening as they walked into the house. Binnie stood up from the sofa with a wide smile. "I hope you had a good evening. Your babies have been asleep for a while now."

"Maybe we should hire you every night," Gavin joked.

Binnie shrugged her shoulders. "They were perfect. I read a few extra books to Sam, but then he was out flat. Proves he had good exercise earlier in the day," she said, nodding in approval toward Sara.

"Thank you for everything," Sara said.

"Anytime," Binnie said. "I fill in when Princess Bridget needs me, but I often have openings. Your children are lovely."

"Thank you," Gavin said. "We're very grateful and

we'll call you again." He stepped forward and pressed cash into Binnie's hand.

She shot him a confused look. "This is not necessary. I've been paid by the palace."

"Not enough," he said. "Please accept my gratitude."

Binnie dipped her head. "You do too much, but thank you," she said, and then she headed out the door.

It was just the two of them in the den again and Sara was taunted by her awareness of Gavin. Meeting her gaze, he shrugged out of his jacket, loosened his tie and unbuttoned the top of his shirt. "Would you like a glass of wine?"

Sara knew that if she stayed, she would be wanting more than a glass of wine. Her lips burned as she remembered his kisses. For a moment, she wanted to ignore all the warnings and cautions running through her mind. Even though she knew that an intimate relationship with Gavin would eventually produce disastrous results, she felt impatient with the deprivation she'd suffered the past few years. Not to mention having to deny her identity, deny her relationship with her sister and deny herself since she'd arrived in Chantaine.

Oh, heaven help her. She was starting to sound like Tabitha.

Biting her lip, she stepped away from the cliff and shook her head. "I think it would be best if I stick with my water and go to bed."

He nodded as if he'd expected her answer. "Good night, then. I had a good time."

"So did I," she said, wanting to be honest about *something.*

"Who knows," he said. "Maybe we can do it again sometime."

Sara heard the sexy tone in his voice and knew she should put the kibosh on that possibility, but something inside didn't let her.

Chapter Seven

Sam didn't attend preschool the next day, so Sara took both children for a long walk despite the cloudy weather. She wanted to beat the impending rain. Sam appeared even more quiet and withdrawn than ever.

Sitting down on the floor with him as he rolled his cars over the edge of the carpet, she pushed one of the cars next to his. "Which do you like better?" she asked. "The blue one or the red one?"

He just shrugged.

Sara pressed her lips together in concern. "What are you thinking about right this minute?"

He shrugged again, then sighed. "I wish Mama was here."

Sara's heart nearly broke in two. She knew she shouldn't expect Sam's healing to take place so quickly, but she had hoped the dazzle of the holidays might distract him from his pain. She reached toward him, then paused. He might not want a hug from her at the moment. "I know you love and miss her. You have a wonderful, loving heart. How could you not miss her? But your mother is always with you. She will live on in your memories and her love for you forever."

Sam looked at her solemnly with wide brown eyes. "I just wish I could see her," he said.

Sara softly touched his arm to comfort him and he allowed it. She racked her brain for another way to comfort him. She remembered the huge Christmas tree in the palace foyer from her childhood days. Loaded with exquisite China and crystal antique ornaments, the tree had also featured antique sterling silver frames of gloomy-looking ancestors from centuries gone by.

Sam's mother wasn't gloomy-looking. She'd worn her hair in a short perky style and although the woman had looked a little weary around the eyes, she'd smiled for the camera. Sara had seen a photograph of the woman on Sam's dresser.

"How about we put a photo of your mother on the Christmas tree?" she said.

"How?" he asked, his eyes widening in curiosity.

"We can make a copy of the photo in your bedroom and put it in a small frame and hang it on the tree. She can be your Christmas angel," she added impulsively.

Sam nodded. "Can we do it now?"

"As soon as Adelaide wakes up from her nap and we eat lunch," she said, pleased if this would provide him a little relief from his grief.

"I can wake her up now," he said, standing.

Sara laughed. "There's no need to do that. Let's get the photo of your mother from your dresser so we'll be ready when it's time to go."

Sam darted for his room and returned in less than a minute, tightly clutching the photo of his mother. "I'm ready," he said.

"Soon," she told him. "We'll leave soon."

As it turned out, Adelaide awakened early, so Sara fed the children their lunches, and then they took off in search of a local office supply shop. She found one easily enough and gave instructions on resizing the photograph. She and Sam chose a small photo frame and since they were already downtown, she took them for gelato.

It took far more coordination than she'd anticipated to prevent Sam from spilling his cup of gelato at the same time she tried to respond to Adelaide's impatient squawks for more. "Tilt your cup up just a bit, Sam," she said, then turned to Adelaide. "Just a second, our queen," she said and pushed the cold confection into the baby's mouth.

"Well, what do we have here," a familiar voice said from behind her. Sara whipped around with Adelaide in her arms and stared into her sister's eyes. "Tab—"

"Jane," her sister corrected and Sara immediately embraced her with Adelaide squirming between them.

"What a treat to get to see you," Sara said. "I've called a few times."

Tabitha's gaze slid away. "I know. I've been busy at the restaurant and a little sad due to the season."

"I know what you mean," Sara said. "Alexander..."

Tabitha nodded. "Yes and I'm growing very weary of—" She broke off and lowered her voice. "All the hiding."

"I feel the same way, but we've got to try to hold on longer. I hope things will change soon."

"I wish I shared your hope."

Sara studied her sister and noticed shadows beneath her eyes. Her face appeared thinner. "Are you sure you're okay? You look a little off."

"Well, thank you very much," Tabitha mocked. "Are you sure it's not the blue streaks in my hair?"

Sara blinked. "I was so focused on your face I didn't notice them."

Adelaide began to kick impatiently. She pointed at the cup of gelato Tabitha held.

Tabitha smiled. "A girl after my own heart. Never be afraid to ask for what you want," she said to Adelaide.

Sara picked up the cup from the table and offered the baby a spoonful of the melting gelato. "Jane," she said before clearing her throat. Sara didn't think she'd ever get used to calling her sister by that name. "Please meet Sam and Adelaide."

Tabitha ruffled Adelaide's curls then knelt down to Sam's level. "It's my pleasure to meet you, Sam. Is that your favorite gelato I see on your face?" she asked. She pulled out a napkin to dab at his chin.

He nodded, staring at Jane. "You look like Miss Sara," he said. "With blue hair."

Tabitha chuckled. "Aren't you the observant one?" she said as she stood. "I can see you have your hands full with these two," she said to Sara. "I'll let you get back to your little darlings."

Reluctant to see her sister leave, Sara stepped toward her. "Promise me you'll return my next call."

"All right, all right," her sister said. "I've missed you. I've just been moping and didn't want to spread my gloom to you."

"We've only got each other right now," she whispered.

"And even that's a bit tricky at the moment," her sister said, twisting her mouth in a frown.

"Are you sure there's nothing else wrong?" Sara asked. Her instincts about her sister were sounding an alarm. "What about your Greek friend?"

Tabitha's gaze slid downward again. "He was just for fun. Easy come, easy go. I really should leave. Ta-ta for now." She brushed a kiss on Sara's cheek, then she quickly walked out of the shop.

Sara stared after her. She felt Sam tug on her pants leg. Glancing down, she saw that his cheeks and chin were covered with the remainder of his chocolate gelato. He looked as if he'd tried to press his entire face into the small bowl to get every last bite. "Oh, dear," she said, reaching for a napkin to wipe his face. "You even got it on your nose," she said, smiling. "I suppose you didn't like it very much at all."

"I want some more," he said with far more enthusiasm than he usually exhibited.

"Another time." She gave Adelaide two more bites. Adelaide reached for the spoon, but Sara successfully dodged her. "All done," she said and tossed their cups and napkins into the trash. "Let's go pick up your mother's picture so we can hang it on the tree."

Sam walked alongside her, glancing up at her. "That girl sounded like you," he said. "She talks like you do."

"She does?" Sara said. "How interesting that you would notice. You must have a very good ear. You clearly have an aptitude for music," she said, changing the subject. She put Adelaide into her car seat, then helped Sam into his.

"And she looks like you 'cept with blue hair," he said.

Sara looked at him and chuckled in frustration. She would have sworn that Sam had paid very little attention to her. Perhaps she'd underestimated him. She'd clearly also underestimated how much she and her sister resembled each other if a four-year-old could spot it.

After picking up the photo, she drove back to the cottage, changed Adelaide and put her down for a nap. She found Sam staring at the photo of his mother when she returned to the den. The longing on his face stabbed at her.

He must have sensed her presence because he looked up at her and stood. "Can we put her on the tree like you said? So she can be our Christmas angel?"

"Of course we can," she said. "Where would you like to put her?"

"Right there," he said pointing just above the middle of the tree.

"Then let me get a chair. I'll hold the chair steady while you hang the ornament." She pulled a chair beside the tree, lifted Sam onto the chair and held on to him to make sure he didn't fall.

Biting his lip in concentration, Sam leaned forward and carefully hung the ornament.

"Perfect," she said, returning him to the floor.

Sam gave a nod of satisfaction. "I'll show Daddy when he gets home."

"I'm sure he'll be very proud of you," she said, hoping she'd finally helped Sam a little with his grieving process.

Gavin pulled into the driveway and sighed. Long day. Complications with the project. The next few days would be jam-packed with him trying to keep everything on schedule. Stefan, the ruling prince of Chantaine, was a stickler for remaining on schedule. Gavin couldn't help admiring the man for wanting the best for his country, but he might just as well stay at the office overnight for all the hours it would take to fulfill Stefan's expectations.

On the bright side, he hoped he'd be too tired to think about how much he wanted his children's nanny in his bed. He shook his head at himself, still surprised at the force of his desire. He'd thought the deadness inside him would last forever. A part of him felt the sting of guilt. What was wrong with him? He should still be grieving.

And he was, but he'd been grieving for years over the distance between him and Lauren, his late wife. He'd been so determined to make it work between them. There'd had to be a way. He would find a way, he'd told Lauren and himself over and over.

Shaking off the heaviness of his thoughts, he walked inside the house and inhaled the scent of spaghetti sauce wafting from the kitchen. He barely made it through the door when Sam ran straight toward him.

"Daddy! Daddy!"

Pleased by Sam's display of enthusiasm, Gavin dropped his hard-shell computer case onto the floor and caught his son up into his arms. "Whoa there," Gavin said. "Where's the fire?"

Sam frowned in confusion. "Fire?"

Gavin shook his head. "What's got you so excited?"

"Miss Sara and I made an angel for the Christmas tree. Come see," he said, wiggling to be set free.

Gavin set him down on the floor and allowed himself

to be led to the den where the awful white tree stood. "Where's the angel?" he asked. Then he saw the photo of Sam's mother hanging on the tree limb.

"Mommy can be our Christmas angel. This way, she can look over us and she won't miss Christmas," Sam said.

Sam's earnestness stabbed him straight in his heart. If only there'd been some way to prevent Lauren's accident. She would be with the kids for Christmas. She might not have been in love with him anymore, but she'd loved those kids. He'd often wondered what he could have done to see the light of love return to her eyes.

Moving to North Dakota had been hard on her. It was almost as if the snow had turned her heart to ice when it came to Gavin. He'd put in for a transfer with his company, but it just hadn't happened soon enough.

"Do you like it, Daddy?" Sam asked.

"You did a great job." He ruffled Sam's soft hair. "Your mom would be proud of you."

"That's what Miss Sara said about you," Sam said. "That you'd be proud of me."

"And I am," he said.

Sara entered the room carrying Adelaide on her hip. She looked from Sam to Gavin.

"I showed Daddy that Mommy is our Christmas angel," Sam said.

He felt Sara searching his face for his reaction, but Gavin was feeling too many things. Most of them painful. "I'll read to Adelaide and Sam after dinner, then I need to do some work at home tonight. There have been a few complications in the project."

"Okay. I've heated up the spaghetti sauce the housekeeper prepared. We can eat anytime."

"Sounds good. Let's clean up, Sam." He then walked down the hall with his son.

Sara looked after Gavin as he went down the hall, feeling a strange mixture of emotions. Good. He was going to be busy working, so he wouldn't have time to seduce her. That was exactly what she wanted. Right?

Adelaide fussed and Sara jiggled her as she returned to the kitchen to put her in her infant seat so Sara could serve the meal. Playing peek-a-boo every other minute, Sara got the meal on the table just before Sam and Gavin appeared.

Sam and Gavin devoured the meal while Sara fed Adelaide. Gavin cleaned up the dishes and Sam took a bath while Sara rushed to bathe Adelaide. Sara stayed just outside the den while Gavin read three books to the children. Adelaide squirmed and squawked through all three books.

After the stories, Gavin picked up Adelaide and urged Sam down the hallway. He handed Adelaide to her. "Do you know what's wrong with her?"

"I think she's teething. I'll get a cold cloth for her," she said, taking the baby.

"I'll put Sam to bed and check on her later," he said.

"That will work. I'll keep an ear out for her, too," she said.

Gavin walked away and Sara felt the distance growing between them. It was what she wanted, she told herself. She needed the distance to stay on track.

It took an hour before Adelaide settled down, and then Sara took a quick shower and collapsed on her bed. She didn't even try to read or listen to music. The day had been exhausting. Her mind spun with thoughts about Gavin. She wanted him. She didn't want to want him. This was for the best. If that was true, then why did she suddenly feel so empty?

Sara rolled over several times and sighed, then adjusted her covers. Staring into the darkness, she finally fell asleep over thirty minutes later. A sound broke through her slumber and she blinked. Adelaide's cry vibrated throughout the cottage. Sara quickly scrambled from her bed to get the baby. Bleary-eyed, she ran into Gavin just outside Adelaide's door.

She instinctively clutched at him to keep from falling. His warm skin was bare and she could feel his muscles tense at her touch. His hands closed around her arms and his chest pressed against hers. Her heart pounded in her chest when she realized that if she weren't wearing her nightgown, there would be nothing between them. Just skin on skin. For one moment out of time, she craved that more than anything.

Gavin must have come to his senses first, still holding her arms yet pulling back. "Are you all right?" he asked in a whisper with a sexy edge of roughness.

Sara swallowed over her suddenly tight throat and nodded. "Yes. I'm sorry. I didn't see you in the dark."

"It's okay," he said, removing his hands. "I need to check on Adelaide."

"Of course," Sara said. "I will, too."

As soon as she entered the room, Sara could see that Adelaide was sitting in her crib with her fingers stuffed in her mouth, wailing at the top of her lungs. "Oh, poor thing. It's her gums."

Gavin scooped up his baby daughter and murmured

low, comforting words to her. "Hey, sweetie, it's okay. We'll take care of you. We'll make you feel better." He glanced toward Sara. "A plan?"

"I have a washcloth ready in the freezer," she said and extended her arms. "I can take her so you can sleep."

Gavin met her gaze. "You need sleep, too, don't you?"

"I can nap when the children do," she said. "You can't."

He gave a slow nod. "Are you sure?"

"I'll let you know when I'm not sure," she said, and she took Adelaide into her arms. The baby gave another pitiful moan. "Go to bed," she urged. "You need your rest. You said you're going to be busy for the next few days." She jiggled Adelaide as the baby fussed.

Gavin kissed his baby on her forehead. "Let me know if you need help."

"Of course," Sara said, but she wouldn't dream of it. She and Adelaide were headed for that washcloth in the freezer. She planned to replace that one with another so it would be ready when they needed a fresh one.

Sara let Adelaide rest against her chest as she munched on the cold washcloth. She fell asleep then awakened to a wet sensation on her upper chest. The dampness was a result of the combination of the washcloth and Adelaide's drool.

Sara made a secret grimace then carefully stood. She went to the sink and rinsed out the washcloth and exchanged her cloth with the frozen one. Walking down the hall, she went to the nursery and carefully set Adelaide into her crib. The baby wiggled a little, but seemed to settle down. Sara waited, poised with the cold washcloth, but Adelaide slept.

Seizing the moment, Sara went to her bed and fell

asleep as soon as her head hit the pillow. Morning came way too early, but she couldn't slack off. Sam was due at preschool and she would need to feed both children right away. Promising herself a shower later in the day, she pulled her hair into a knot at the base of her nape, stuck some hair pins in it, washed her face and brushed her teeth, then pulled on some clothes.

Heading for Adelaide's room since she heard the baby crying, she stopped as Gavin walked out of the nursery with the baby in his arms. Already dressed for work, he allowed Adelaide to gnaw on his finger, wincing when she bit down.

Sympathy shot through Sara. "Baby teeth are sharp," she said, commiserating.

"A lot like puppies and kittens," he said. "I wish I could stay and help with her, but I'm slammed."

"That's why I'm here," she said, reaching for Adelaide. "We'll be fine."

"Don't hold dinner for me tonight. I'll probably be late," he said.

Sara nodded. "The housekeeper is supposed to come this afternoon. I'm sure she'll bring some food, too. I'll just set some aside for you in the refrigerator. Good luck with the project."

He met her gaze for several seconds, then looked away. "Call me if there's an emergency. Perhaps we should ask the sitter who took care of the kids that night if she can come and give you some relief."

"I can handle it. Saturday is my day off, remember?" she said.

"That's right," he said. "Good luck with the teeth."

He pressed a kiss on Adelaide's head and ruffled

Sam's hair as the boy wandered out of his room. "I'll see you tonight, bud. Be good for Miss Sara."

Sara watched him leave until Adelaide began to fuss.

"I don't wanna go to school today," Sam said.

"You only have a few more days of school before you get three weeks off for Christmas break. Besides, I bet you're going to be doing lots of fun holiday activities and might even get some special holiday treats."

"Treats?" he said, his brown eyes lighting with interest.

"Yes," she said. "Who knows? You may even find a special treat with your snack today."

"I get cheese or fruit for my snack. I never get treats," he said.

"Well, maybe you will today," she said, deciding to pack a small piece of chocolate with Sam's snack. She didn't want to bribe him to go to school, but she wanted him to have a positive association. If a little piece of candy helped, then she was all for it.

The rest of the day passed in a blur of activity. Adelaide fussed off and on while Sara dragged her around to run a few errands. When she picked up Sam, she learned he'd not only eaten the chocolate she'd packed for him, he'd also consumed three cookies. His sugar high made him too hyper to take a nap at his regular time, but he finally settled down.

Sara rested on the den sofa, but never quite fell asleep. The naps extended longer than she expected and she hesitated to wake the children. More than ever, she now understood the advice to never wake sleeping babies.

Still, she grew concerned when thirty extra minutes had passed, so she tiptoed down the hall and noticed Sam's door was wide open and Sam was not in his bed. She walked farther down the hall and saw the nursery door open. Sara heard low sounds of laughter and delight.

Well, it couldn't be too bad if no one was screaming. Right?

Sara pushed open the door to the sight of Sam coloring Adelaide's face with a green marker.

She blinked. "Sam!"

He turned and she saw that he had also colored himself with a marker.

"What are you doing?" she asked.

"I'm a frog," he said as he jumped up and down. "Adelaide is a turtle. She's slow."

Sara sighed. "Well, that certainly explains it." She bit her lip, wondering *how* she was going to get the marker off both of them.

Thank goodness the markers were washable. She bathed both of the children while the housekeeper arrived with food and did laundry. Laundry and cooking weren't Sara's forte. She could put together a sandwich or reheat something as long as she wasn't in a rush. She'd been known to burn food. As for laundry, she didn't trust herself with much more than linens.

Before she knew it, she'd fed the children and read three books to them. Adelaide fell asleep quickly, but Sam was determined to wait up for his father. Sara tried to coax him into bed, but Sam's eyes welled with threatening tears. Sara decided not to fight the boy on it. Sam's number one source of security and stability was his father.

Gavin finally walked through the front door, his steps heavy from his long day. Sam perked up from playing with his plastic blocks and ran straight for his father.

"Hey, bud, what are you doing up? Isn't this past your bedtime?" Gavin shot a questioning glance at Sara.

"Sam knows we have to make a habit of a regular bedtime, but it seemed especially important to him to see you tonight before he went to sleep," she said.

Gavin met her gaze and she suspected he might ask her to elaborate later. For now, he reached down and picked up his son in his arms. "Well, tell me about your day while I grab a sandwich."

"There's some soup for you in a bowl. I can heat it up in the microwave," she offered.

"Thanks. I'd appreciate it," he said.

Sara felt a tug every time she looked at him. The sensation bothered her. It appeared as if he had reined in his desire for her. Why couldn't she do the same for him?

Chapter Eight

"This can't go on forever," Sara promised herself when Adelaide's cries awakened her at two in the morning. Again. She scooped up the baby from her crib and headed down the hallway

Gavin opened his bedroom door and she waved him away. "I've got her."

"Are you sure?" he asked, walking to her side.

The sight of him shirtless only served to amp up her irritation. Not only was she sleep deprived, she was feeling sex deprived. Of all the times for her to start feeling her oats, this had to be the worst. "I'm fine."

"You look extremely tired," he said.

"I am," she admitted. "But I'm strong. I can handle this."

"I wasn't suggesting that you're weak. I just—"

She waved her hand for him to stop. "I'll be fine.

That tooth will come through Adelaide's gum and we'll all have a party. After we sleep," she added.

Gavin gave a slight chuckle and shook his head. "I gotta hand it to you. You're keeping your sense of humor."

"Well, thank you. Now back to bed," she said.

"If we have another night like this, I'm getting some backup. I've been reluctant to bring anyone else in because both the children seem so at ease with you."

"Again, thank you, but let's just get through tonight first. No need to borrow trouble," she said. She felt as if she'd been living under that mantra nonstop for too many months. Sara's patience with her secrets and worries about her missing brother were stretching her thin. She'd always been calm and steady, but she was finding it more and more difficult.

"Now please go to bed," she said. It was on the tip of her tongue to add, *Because staring at your naked chest is making me think about what I've never had but suddenly need.*

Sara pulled a frozen washcloth from the freezer for the baby then poured herself a glass of water. With the image of Gavin stamped on her brain, she seriously considered dumping the water down her shirt to cool off her libido.

The next day, Sara hit a wall and decided to take a rest at the same time the children went down for their naps. She kept her door open and set an alarm to awaken her since she felt as if she could sleep for a good four hours instead of just one.

A horrible loud beeping sound jerked her from her sleep and she awakened to the sight and smell of smoke rolling into her room. Panic shot through her. *Fire.* For one moment, she was six years old and back in the palace, blinded by the thick smoke. Panic froze her in place.

She blinked it away and shook her head. She wasn't six and this wasn't the palace. *The children.* Fear gave her legs. She had to get the children out of the house.

Running into the hallway, she noticed the smoke was thicker toward the nursery and the laundry room. Her heart caught in her throat. Adelaide. Please let her be okay, she prayed. Despite the encroaching smoke, the baby slept soundly. Sara, however, had experience with the aftereffects of smoke inhalation. Snatching the baby from her crib, she automatically grabbed the diaper bag.

Sam appeared in the hallway with his hands covering his ears. "What's happening?"

"There's a fire. We have to get out of the house," she said. "We have to go now," she said, urging him down the hallway. "Quick, quick, quick like a bunny."

"I'm not a bunny. I'm a frog," he told her.

"You're right," she said, remembering how he'd colored his body and Adelaide's with green markers. "How could I forget?"

"But what about my toys?" he protested.

"We can't worry about the toys. We have to get out." She grabbed his hand and pulled him into the den where the smoke was beginning to spread. "Out the door." She remembered to grab her keys and cell phone.

"But what about the Christmas angel?" he asked, his eyes full of fright. "We have to get the Christmas angel."

"Of course, you're right," she said, pulling the ornament from the tree. Stuffing it into the diaper bag, she pushed open the door and took Sam's hand again.

"Where are we going?" he asked.

"To the car." Sara plopped Adelaide into her car seat then helped Sam into his. With trembling hands, she called emergency. A woman answered the phone. "We have a fire," she said. "There's a fire in our house. It's filled with smoke."

"What is your address?" the woman asked.

Still rattled, she managed to give the woman the information and was told a fire truck was on its way. Immediately afterward, she called Gavin. He didn't answer, so she left a scrambled message. She then called Tabitha and assured her sister repeatedly that she and the children were safe. After she hung up from Tabitha, she called Princess Ericka.

"There's a fire in the cottage. The children and I are in the car," she babbled.

"That's terrible," Princess Ericka said. "We'll take care of you. Don't worry. Have you contacted Gavin?

"He didn't answer," Sara said. "He said this was a busy week.

"Stefan can be such a slave driver," she muttered. "I'll take care of this. Sit tight."

"The fire trucks have arrived," Sara said, watching as the screaming trucks pulled into the driveway.

"Excellent."

"But I'm going to need formula soon," Sara said.

"I understand. We'll take care of you. Call me in ten minutes," Ericka said before she hung up.

Sara tamped down her anxiety attack by taking several breaths. "Well, isn't that fire engine impressive, Sam? What do you think of the siren?"

Sam frowned and covered his ears. "It's too loud."

"It's loud so it can warn people that it's coming,"

she said. "Having a fire engine come to your house is a big deal."

Sam uncovered his ears. "It is?"

"It definitely is." She wished her hands would stop shaking.

Adelaide gave a sound of protest.

Sara pulled her from her seat and put the baby on her lap. "How do you like all this excitement?"

Adelaide looked up at Sara as if she were a crazy woman. Perhaps she was.

"I want some juice," Sam said.

Sara shook her head. "We don't have any. We have to pretend we're in the desert and we can get some later."

"Do we have any cookies?" he asked.

Sara shook her head again as she watched the firemen enter the cottage with hoses pumped full of water. "I'll give you three cookies tonight."

"Three?" he echoed. "I had three at school yesterday."

"Three cookies and a large cup of juice are in your future. I just need you to hang on and help entertain Adelaide."

"Do we have any markers?" he asked. "She liked being a turtle."

"I have no markers," Sara said, relieved that she was speaking the truth. "Maybe you can make faces and noises at her."

Watching the firefighters enter the cottage, she leaned her head back against the headrest. She heard Sam making weird noises and tried to calm her heart and breathing. This wasn't the same as the time she'd nearly suffocated at the palace when she was a child. This was totally different.

Sara took several more breaths.

Sam made a noise. Adelaide giggled.

All was good, she told herself. The firefighters seemed to be quenching the fire. *Good*, she thought. That was good.

Several moments later, one of the men approached her and she lowered her window. "Everything okay here?" he asked.

"We're going to need some formula and clothes," she said.

"And toys and the tree," Sam shouted. "We need our Christmas tree."

The man twitched his lips. "We'll work on that. We can't let you back in yet, but we can gather a few things for you. Can you give us directions?"

"Of course," Sara said. "But first, how did the fire start?"

"Looks like the laundry room," he said. "Were you doing any laundry today?"

Sara shook her head. "No."

"Unfortunately some of these older cottages have wiring issues, especially in the laundry area."

"That's frightening," she said.

The man nodded. "We're trying to bring everyone up to code, but it takes a bit of time."

She gave a slow nod, still feeling her own set of jitters. "We will need clothing," she said.

"It's going to smell like smoke," he said.

"We can air it out or clean it," she countered. "Can you please let me go inside?"

"It's against regulations," he said, clearly reluctant.

"I promise I won't take long," she said. "But I will want one of your men to remain here with the children."

"Okay," he said. "Deal." He waved one of his men over and escorted Sara into the cottage. The stench of smoke nearly overwhelmed her, but she was determined to cover it. She placed her hand over her mouth.

Trying to keep her mind clear, she grabbed diapers and clothing for Adelaide. Then she scooped up some clothing from her own room and from Sam's. She grabbed a few extra toys, the sound machine, and she gathered some clothing from Gavin's bedroom, too. She noticed a laptop and added that to the pile.

"Formula," she said to the fireman and pulled out a few bottles from the refrigerator, along with some cookies.

Sara looked at the tree. "Sam really wants the tree."

"We'll put it on the porch," he said. "We need to get out."

"I think that's the best I can do," she said and walked toward the door.

"Do you need some shoes?" he asked.

Sara looked down at her bare feet and chuckled. "I guess so." She returned to her room and collected shoes for herself and the children, then walked out the front door with the fireman.

It could have been worse. So very much worse.

Just as she loaded several things into the trunk of the car, Gavin pulled into the driveway. He raced from his car. "Thank God, you're all right."

Sara felt a sliver of relief, and it was all she could do not to sink into his arms. "The children are fine," she said.

Gavin touched Sam and Adelaide as if he wanted to be sure. Then he turned to Sara and shook his head.

"This must have been horrible for you. Especially after that fire you experienced when you were a child."

She couldn't deny it, but she tried. Sara shook her head. "It wasn't that bad. The smoke alarm saved us. Sam was wonderful. He followed my directions."

Gavin put his arms around her and held her, and Sara couldn't find the strength to pull away. She slumped against him. "We have formula and clothing and the fireman said he would put the terrible tree on the porch if we really want it. Apparently Sam has grown attached to it."

Gavin squeezed her tighter, then chuckled. "I guess we'll be staying in a hotel tonight."

"Maybe," Sara said. Her cell phone rang and she pulled back and accepted the call. "Sara," she said.

"Sara, this is Ericka. We're all horrified about the fire. The good news is there's plenty of room at the palace. We've arranged for you to stay there as long as necessary."

"Oh, thank you," Sara said. "We really appreciate this. I hate that the children will be disrupted again, but I think it would be a stable environment for them."

"Yes, it will," Ericka said. "We have a nanny ready to take over for the next few nights. You will need some time to recover."

"I'm fine," Sara said.

"Of course you are. You're a royal. You're always fine. That said, we would like to help you and Gavin recover."

Humbled, Sara felt tears swell. "Thank you. You are too kind."

"You would do the same," Ericka said. "Ciao for now. Call me for anything."

Gavin looked at her with a questioning glance. "Well?"

"What do you think about staying at the palace for a while?" she said.

He blinked. "The palace?"

"Yes, with a nanny to help us," she said.

"I'll take it," he said, glancing back at his children. "What about the ugly Christmas tree?"

"We'll figure it out," she said. "Let's strap in the babies and get to the palace."

As soon as they all arrived at the palace, Sara felt reluctant to hand over the children. She wanted them safe and secure. When Sam started running in circles demanding cookies and Adelaide filled a diaper, she got over her trepidation. After changing Adelaide, she handed the baby over to Binnie who took Sam, as well.

Then she went to her new quarters, took a shower and collapsed on her plush bed. Hours later, she awakened to a tray of food in the room on a stand. She lifted the tin from the soup and found it still warm, along with a covered dish of chicken and vegetables.

Sara gobbled half of it down and stretched on the bed in pleasure. She felt as if she'd gone back in time to when staff had prepared her food and served it at any time of night or day. These days were different, but, oh, this was a delightful temporary change.

She sank back on the bed for at a few moments, then thought of Sam and Adelaide. She had to check on them. Pulling on a robe, she stepped from her bed to the hallway. She'd been told the nursery was just down the hall. Walking toward the suite, she stopped outside and pressed her ear against the door. Hearing nothing, she carefully pushed the door open and found no one in the entryway.

Seconds later Binnie appeared with her index finger pressed to her lips. "They're both asleep. It took the boy a bit longer."

"He may have still been a little upset by the fire," Sara said.

"Yes," Binnie said. "But he's out for the count now."

"Good," Sara said. "If either of them need me…" she began.

"They should sleep long and well," Binnie said. "They've had an eventful day."

"Still," Sara said.

Binnie smiled. "You're more than a nanny. You're like a mother. I'll call you if they need you."

Sara felt her heart shift at the woman's words. Like a mother? "Thank you," she managed.

"Get some rest," Binnie said. "You deserve it. You're quite the hero."

Sara shook her head. "I bumbled though."

"You bumbled quite well," Binnie corrected. "To bed you go now."

Sara nodded, then returned to her room and slept the whole night through. The next morning, she arose, ready to fulfill her duties as nanny. The Devereaux family, however, had different plans.

Binnie greeted her as she entered the nursery. "The palace has determined that you should take some rest. You are to take the next two days off."

Sara stared at the woman in confusion. "Two days off?"

"Yes," Binnie said. "It was never intended that you should work yourself to exhaustion."

"I'm not exhausted," Sara protested.

The nanny shot her a skeptical glance. "That's debatable."

"I'd still like to see the children," Sara said.

Binnie nodded. "Of course you can." She led Sara into the expansive nursery. Sam played with Lego bricks and Adelaide did her best to crawl across the room.

Sam looked up. "Miss Sara," he said. Then he ran to her and hugged her.

Her heart squeezed tight at his reaction. "It looks like you're having a good day."

"Nanny B says I might get to play with Tyler and Travis," he said, clearly excited.

"That should be fun," she said.

"When will we get our white tree?" he asked.

"I'm not sure," she said. "I thought you didn't like the white tree."

"It's not too bad," he said, returning to his toys.

Adelaide squealed when Sara knelt down on the floor in front of her. "And how are you? How are your gums?"

Adelaide gave a wide smile, revealing her precious teeth.

"I think one just punched through her gums," Binnie said. "She's not drooling as much."

"Thank goodness," Sara said. "I thought she was going to be teething forever."

"This may only be a break," Binnie said. "But she seems happy at the moment."

Adelaide beamed at Sara. "I think you're right."

"Now that you're satisfied that your babies are good and healthy, can you take a rest?"

They're not my babies, she thought, but deep inside her, that didn't ring true. "I'm not sure I could ever be totally satisfied about their health and well-being. However, with you in charge, that's as close as I'll get. Again, I need to know that you'll call me immediately for anything."

"Of course we will. But please, do rest. You're well overdue."

Sara returned to her room and walked around her suite. She was so restless she didn't know what to do with herself. Glancing at the clock, she decided to try for a visit with her sister. She called several times, but Tabitha didn't pick up, so she decided to venture downtown to try to see her.

Climbing the steps to her sister's apartment, Sara knocked on the door, half hoping she wouldn't encounter her Greek Adonis boyfriend.

Sara knocked again and Tabitha finally opened the door, her face pale and her eyes underscored with purple shadows.

Sara gasped. "Are you ill? You look terrible."

"Perhaps," Tabitha said. "Thank you for the compliments."

Sara frowned in concern. "I'm not joking. Are you okay?"

"Most days I am," Tabitha said. "I'm just having a bad day."

"Have you seen a doctor?" Sara asked.

"For what?" Tabitha asked. "Feeling crappy every now and then?"

"Maybe I should take off some time to take care of you," Sara said.

Tabitha lifted a dark eyebrow. "I'm betting I would be more difficult than the children. Besides, don't you need a break after that fire? I was horrified when you called and told me about it."

"I'm okay. It wasn't fun, but everyone's okay. That's what's important. But even though you may be a tiny bit difficult, that doesn't mean I wouldn't want to take care of you if you needed me. Do you mind if I make some tea?"

"Go right ahead. There's hot water in the kettle. And, of course, you would take care of me. You're the Joan of Arc in our family. You don't have to put yourself last and be a martyr all the time."

"After going through two fires, I don't want to be associated with someone who was burned at the stake," Sara said, walking to the small galley kitchen and fixing her cup of tea. "I'm starting to understand your impatience to experience life."

Tabitha followed her and lifted her eyebrows. "Are you having feelings for the baby daddy?"

Sara held her breath.

"Oh, that silence told me everything. I say go for it. You've held back all of your life. This is the time to let it go. But use a condom."

"Tabitha," Sara said in a reproachful voice.

Tabitha lifted her hands. "I offer wisdom when I can. Use a condom."

Sara frowned. "I'm still worried about you. Let me fix you a cup of tea."

"I've already had mine. I'm sure this is just a gastrointestinal virus. Very common in the food-service industry. Remember I'm exposed to the public all the time," Tabitha said.

"But you don't handle food," Sara said and took a sip from her cup.

"Yes, I do," Tabitha said. "I deliver food and occasionally clean tables. So I'm at risk."

"I'd like you to see a doctor," Sara said.

Tabitha shrugged. "In a week. I think this will pass. I'd rather hear news about Alexander."

Sara's heart tightened. "I can't stop thinking about Alexander either. I'm going to press Ericka soon."

"That's unusual coming from you. You've been the one telling me to hold on and be patient," Tabitha said. "I wouldn't have expected it of you."

"It's been a year. We need some news," Sara said, setting her cup on the counter. "If I can't work things out with Ericka, I'll go to Stefan and anyone and everyone else."

Tabitha met her gaze, then looked away. "You're braver than I am."

"I'm not sure about that," Sara said. "I may just be more tired of waiting. My patience has been consumed."

"That's rare coming from you," Tabitha said.

"Maybe I'm learning from you," Sara said.

Tabitha shook her head and gave a rough chuckle. "I hope not. Trust me. You're the better of the two of us. Don't take on my qualities."

"I think that deed is done," Sara said. "I'm starting to think there may be some benefit to being impatient."

Chapter Nine

Sara returned to the palace and checked on the children. Sam was happily playing with the children of Prince Stefan and Eve, and Adelaide was taking a nap. Sara had been so busy the past few weeks that she barely knew what to do with herself now that the children were temporarily under another nanny's care.

Returning to her room, she saw a note had been left on her bedside table. Scanning the note from Princess Ericka, she smiled at how conscientious and caring the princess was. The cottage would be emptied within the next day so that as much clothing as possible could be aired out from the smoke and cleaned if necessary. Ericka planned to have another residence ready for Gavin and the children in less than a week, and she would make sure the white Christmas tree would be waiting when the family arrived. In the meantime, she hoped Ericka would take a well-earned rest and enjoy the use of a piano tucked away in a back room on the third floor. Day or night, Ericka said. It was a soundproof room.

Sara's heart melted at Ericka's sweet attentiveness. All of the Devereaux family had been wonderful to her and Tabitha. She closed her eyes. The trouble was that they had no news from Alex.

Sinking onto her bed, she sighed. She needed to do something soon. Images of Alex flashed through her mind. The night of that fire, he'd gathered her tightly against him after she'd been rescued with the help of a guard. She hadn't felt the terrible burn on her palms until she'd leaned against him.

She felt the clock ticking. How long should she wait? Alex had probably wondered how long he would be forced to wait before he was allowed to reenter the palace that had been full of the flames and fires keeping Sara captive. Waiting didn't feel right. She started thinking about how to approach Princess Ericka and Prince Stefan if it became necessary. For Sara, it was a matter of days, not weeks, at this point.

Sara decided to get some ideas for the children's Christmas gifts online. She would consult with Gavin, but they needed to make plans. She visited the children for dinner and fed Adelaide. Thank goodness, her tooth really had come through. She was the happiest baby ever. Sara knew, however, that another bout of sore gums was in the future. She just hoped it wasn't as bad as the last one.

She took a walk around the palace twice, then returned to her room, took a shower and ate the meal that appeared in her suite. She went to bed and tried to sleep. Tossing and turning, counting down from two hundred, she still couldn't fall asleep. Scowling, Sara arose from her bed and pulled on a robe. Ericka had encouraged Sara to play the piano anytime, so Sara decided to take her up on the offer. She prayed she wouldn't awaken anyone.

Taking the stairs down to the third floor, she wandered through the halls and finally found the soundproof room with the piano. Sara felt a sensation of relief at the sight of it as she closed the door behind her and approached the instrument.

Sliding onto the bench, she lifted her fingers to the keys and tested the sound and sensation. It was better tuned than the piano she'd played at the cottage, and she began to play a piece by Bach. The exercise and sound soothed her, so she segued into another by Mozart. She followed with Beethoven, then performed a tune from a musical. She took a quick breath then heard the sound of applause from behind her.

She whipped around to find Gavin sitting in a chair clapping his hands.

"What—"

"I got the same note from Princess Ericka," he said. "I couldn't find you in your suite, so I came looking for you. I didn't expect to hear a professional concert."

"You flatter me," she said because she knew she was a bit out of practice.

"I don't," Gavin said, rising from his chair and walking toward her. "You haven't been completely honest with me."

Sara's stomach clenched.

"I wish you weren't so afraid," he said. "I wish you felt you could trust me, but I know it can be hard to trust."

Sara sighed. "It won't be this way forever," she whispered.

She felt the connection between them deepen as

Gavin squeezed her shoulder. Then he touched her face. "You are so beautiful, inside and out."

Sara closed her eyes. "You are very kind." She smiled. She opened her eyes and the expression on Gavin's face captured every cell of her.

He lowered his mouth to hers, taking her in a kiss that grabbed at every part of her. Sara felt need and want in a way she'd never experienced before. He pulled her up from the bench of the piano.

Gavin slid his hands over her shoulders, then down her arms. "Stop me soon," he said against her mouth. "I could have lost you in that fire. I haven't been able to stop thinking about that. I want to make love to you."

Sara's heart skipped. She clung to him as she considered what he was asking of her. Her heart and her body couldn't deny her need and want, but her mind… Her mind told her to wait… Take some time…don't rush…

But there was something inside her that wouldn't wait. Life was short.

She slid her hands over his jaw and drew him into a deep kiss. He met her stroke for stroke and his need kindled hers. She pulled back.

"No stopping," she said breathlessly.

Gavin scooped her up from the piano bench and carried her from the room down the stairs to his suite. He set her on his bed and followed her down. "I feel like I've been waiting for you forever," he said.

Still a little nervous, she wrapped her hands around his neck and drowned herself in his delicious kiss. She felt his hand caress her body. He kissed her jaw, neck, throat. Gavin touched her breasts and pushed away her robe and nightgown. He slid his lips down her throat to her breasts.

Sara arched against him, wanting more. Her body was on fire. In just a moment, he'd touched off her pleasure points.

"Oh, Sara," he said. "You feel so good."

He slid his hand between her legs and continued to kiss her deeply.

Sara wriggled beneath him, sliding her hands over his back and backside. The intimacy caught her off guard, but she had to go further. She had to rub against him. She had to feel him. Inside and out. Sara slid her fingers through his hair.

She felt him rubbing himself against her. Sara was consumed with the need to have him inside her.

"I want you," she whispered, wriggling against him.

"Give me a second," he said as he pulled on protection. Then he thrust inside her.

Sara's eyes opened in surprise. Her body froze. He was too big. She was too tight.

Gavin stared at her, huffing and puffing. "You're a virgin. Why didn't you tell me?" he asked.

"I didn't think it would matter," she managed and made an experimental slide. "That's better," she said.

Gavin clenched his teeth. "You think so? Stop moving or—"

Sara wriggled again. "Ooh, that feels good."

"Stop," Gavin said.

But she couldn't help moving. Suddenly he felt so good inside her.

She lifted her hips and Gavin thrust several times. Two moments later, it was all over.

For him.

Gavin pulled her closer to him. Her body continued to pulse in all her pleasure points. Dissatisfaction was not enough of a description for what she felt. She felt annoyance, unanswered need.

Sara sighed. If this was sex, she didn't want any more of it.

"Sorry," Gavin said. "I didn't take care of you. You felt so good. I couldn't wait. It has been so long for me."

Sara took a breath and tried to relax. It didn't quite work, but Gavin's words helped soothe her overly aroused self.

"I can take care of you," he said as he lowered his mouth to hers. He also lowered his hand between her legs and found her where she was swollen and needy.

"You are sweeter than honey," he told her as he stroked her.

Sara felt a tightening sensation deep and low inside her.

"So good," he muttered, continuing to touch her and kiss her deeply at the same time.

Sara felt herself wriggle with the warring sensations of pleasure and frustration.

"Come on," he urged. "Let go." His mouth moved down her body to kiss her and consume her. "I can't get enough of you."

The sensation of his fingers and mouth on her sent her over the edge. She clung to his shoulders, crying. "Gavin."

Seconds later, he thrust inside her again and one, two, three strokes later, they both went over the edge.

Sara rested her head against Gavin's chest. The rhythm of his heartbeat and his arms wrapped around her made her feel safer than she could remember. She had been as close to him as a woman could get, and yet she wanted to be so much closer. She wanted to be rid of the secrets between them. She wanted to be honest with him about who she really was. But she knew she couldn't.

Her brief moment of contentment began to fade and she exhaled on a long breath.

"I'm not looking at your face, but I can feel your brain running a hundred miles an hour. And that sigh—I'd like to believe it was a sigh of pleasure, but I have a feeling it's not. What's bothering you?"

Sara sighed again and looked up at Gavin. "Nothing I can talk about. I'm sorry. I wish I could, but I really can't. It's so frustrating for me, especially now…after we have been so close."

"Do you think you can't trust me?" he asked, his dark brows furrowed in concern.

She reached up to smooth his brow. "It's not that. I believe in you. I've seen what a good father you are. You're a good man."

He pulled her hand to his mouth and kissed it. "That's good to know."

Her heart dipped at his intense expression. "I know it's nearly impossible to understand, but I just really cannot discuss it. There's too much at risk."

"Hmm," he said. "That sounds serious. Are you a secret spy?" he asked with a hint of humor in his eyes.

She shook her head and chuckled. "No, and I'd be a lousy one if I tried to be. That's for sure."

"Your emotions show on your face," he said.

"Not everyone has been able to read me so well. You're different in that way. You're different in a lot of ways."

Gavin pulled her upward as he lowered his mouth to hers in a gentle, soulful kiss. Pleasure flowed through her, along with a sweetness so deep and so wide it nearly brought her to tears.

Sara almost fell asleep in Gavin's arms, but she couldn't help thinking that if one of the children should need her or him, it would be awkward. Another secret, she thought as she slid out of bed and dressed herself.

"Where are you going?"

"Back to my room," she said, feeling him study her face. "I think it would be best not to publicize our relationship. I think it would be confusing for the children, and I don't want the gossip for either you or me."

He rose from the bed, heedless of his glorious nakedness. She kept her gaze on his chin. Otherwise she would have been entirely distracted. He slid his hand under her jaw and gently lifted her chin to look into her eyes.

"Ashamed?"

Sara blinked in surprise. "No," she said, shaking her head. "Not at all. I just don't want to confuse the children. And I want what's between you and me to stay that way. At least for now."

"Okay." He brushed a kiss on her forehead. "I'll walk you to your room," he said.

"Not dressed like that," she retorted.

He chuckled. "You mean undressed," he said.

She felt her cheeks heat and chastised herself. She was a grown woman. She might be inexperienced, but she wasn't completely naive. "You know what I mean. I'll see you in the morning," she said. Then she realized that technically it was already morning. "I mean later." She cleared her throat, then walked to the door.

She put her hand on the doorknob.

"Sara," Gavin said.

Her heart pounded in her throat. She needed to get away from him to regain some of her sanity. He made her feel all fuzzy and out of sorts. "Yes," she said.

"Sweet dreams," he said in a sexy voice that reminded her of the intimacy they'd just shared.

She took a quick breath. "Same to you." She quickly strode to her suite next door. Sliding out of her robe, she got into bed and stared up at the ceiling, her body tense and her eyes wide open. Her heart thumped with a combination of exhilaration and disbelief. What had she done?

Gavin pulled on a pair of pajama bottoms and paced around the suite. He poured a glass of water and downed it in six gulps. He'd known his desire for Sara was powerful, but the strength of his protectiveness for her still surprised him. He could only imagine how terrified she must have felt when the smoke alarm had gone off in the cottage. Yet she hadn't frozen. She'd gotten the children out, called emergency services and contacted the palace. And she'd kept Adelaide and Sam safe.

There were times when he wondered if she was all that strong, but then he saw how she got up night after night with Adelaide when the baby was teething. She persisted with Sam, just nudging him, encouraging him out of his comfort zone.

When she'd appeared on his doorstep, he'd dismissed her as too young for the job and also too young for him. But she'd shown him different sides of herself. She reminded him of a deep, deep lake. Sara was the definition of the expression "still waters run deep." There was much more to her than met the eye. There was much more than he knew now even after making love to her tonight. He was impatient to know all of her. Her secrecy frustrated him, but he suspected, no, he knew there was nothing devious in her secrecy. She seemed far too tortured about it. He wondered about her brother and if there was any way he could help find him. Would that bring her some peace? Would that help Sara understand that she could trust him? And why was it so important that he convince her? It just felt more important than ever. Especially after he and Lauren had failed.

Even though Gavin knew she was in the next room, he wanted her with him. Her presence soothed something wicked inside him. She radiated hope even though he sensed she struggled with hope herself at times.

Gavin couldn't remember feeling so close to a woman, yet wanting to feel even closer.

Sara finally fell asleep and awakened later than usual. Dragging herself out of bed, she took a shower then decided she should spend some time with her children. Well, Gavin's children. It was complicated.

Despite the fill-in nanny's protests, Sara insisted on taking the children for a walk. She rubbed the baby's gums, then she asked Sam what had been his favorite recent activity.

"The blocks in the nursery. But where's the white tree?" he asked.

"I thought you didn't like the white tree," she said as they walked on a sidewalk around the palace.

"I just want it to be okay," he said.

Sara squeezed his shoulder quickly then moved her hand away. "It's fine. We may see it very soon."

Sam glanced up at her. "When?"

"In a few days," she said.

"Where?" he asked.

"Well, I hear we may be moving into a new house," she said.

"One that won't catch on fire?" Sam asked.

Sara grimaced. "Definitely. Good things are happening."

"When is Daddy gonna play video games with me?" he asked.

Sara's heart dipped. "Maybe on Sunday. We're getting ready to move to a new house, so we have to get things ready. But I think Sunday might work. That's only three sleeps."

Sam sighed. "That's not too long."

"You are so right." Sara noticed he was a bit edgy, so she said, "Run to the corner and back. See if you can beat me there."

Sam ran and she rushed to meet him but he won the race. "Oh, you got me."

"You've got Adelaide. I've just got me," Sam said, breathing hard.

Sara couldn't resist bending down to kiss him on the top of his head. "You're a superhero."

Sam nodded. "I'm a frog."

Sara laughed and hoped the palace kept the markers hidden. She would mention it to Binnie.

Later that night, she and Gavin were served dinner with the children in the nursery. Good thing, given the fact that Sam tossed crumbs from his chicken tenders on the floor and Adelaide spat strained green peas into the atmosphere.

"This is going to take a few minutes to clean up," she said to Gavin.

"You don't say," Gavin as he was caught by a new

green spray from Adelaide. "That's it," he said and lifted his daughter from the high chair. "You're done with dinner, aren't you?

Adelaide gurgled and gave a huge openmouthed, mostly toothless smile.

Gavin hugged her against him, despite the fact that he would get more strained peas on his shirt. "You're my girl," he said. "Now let's clean you up."

Adelaide squawked throughout the cleanup process, but calmed down when he talked quietly to her and took her on a walk.

"I want Daddy," Sam said, anxiously looking after his father and Adelaide.

"He'll come back," Sara promised. "He's just trying to give Adelaide some love. You know how much her gums hurt. But he can't wait to spend some time with you," she said. " He's been working very hard so he can have a break and be with you."

Sam seemed to relax. "Am I s'posed to go back to school?" he asked.

She was surprised he'd asked. "Next week for three days, then you're off."

Sam nodded. "There's gonna be a party with cupcakes next week."

"Well, you wouldn't want to miss that," Sara said. "I bet we'll be in the new house by then."

"Can we have the white tree and Mommy's Christmas angel at the new house?"

"I bet we can." Seeing that Sam was getting restless again, she said, "Hurry. Run across the room until I say stop and then run back," she said. "Go!"

Sam pumped his legs.

"Stop!" she called, and he immediately halted.

"Not at all," Gavin said. "You don't need to stay in here. I just wanted to give the place a last check."

Sara stepped outside onto the small porch, but the smell of smoke still hovered, so she walked to the lane and down the street a bit. Although she'd held herself together when she'd heard the smoke alarm, even now the whole notion that she'd walked out of two fires left her wondering if she was destined to do this again. What was that quote about trouble? It always comes in threes.

Sara shuddered at the thought. For heaven's sake, she hoped not. If this happened again, she was going to wonder if she was cursed. Taking a deep breath, she walked down the block to clear her head.

The neighbor she'd met previously stepped out of his driveway and waved at her. "Hello," he called. "I saw your house caught on fire. I hope everyone is well."

She nodded in return. "We're all fine, thank you." She started to turn around and head back to the house, but the neighbor jogged toward her.

Sara felt a sliver of dread. Every time she saw this man, she was afraid he was going to figure out her true identity. Now was no exception.

He approached her. "I saw the fire trucks, but I think you and the children had already left. Glad you all got out okay."

"Thank you," she said. "It was a frightening experience, but we're all fine."

"You'll be moving back in soon, then?"

Sara shook her head. "The wiring in the house is inferior. We'll be moving to a different house."

"Sorry to see you go," Mr. Trevon said.

"Thank you very much. I wish the best to you," she said, and she began walking toward the cottage.

Sara couldn't help smiling at his response. "Run back. Beat me to the toy box across the room."

Sara raced with him. She targeted that toy box, but Sam arrived first.

"You're a rock star," Sara said breathlessly and lifted her hand for Sam to press his palm against hers. "A frog. The fastest frog in the world."

Sam lifted his arms and roared. "I'm a frog," he yelled.

Sara was so thrilled that Sam was expressing himself in such a powerful way. He was starting to step out of the shadow of his grief. "Roar, Sam. Give a frog roar," she said, and Sam roared back at her.

Sara felt tears sting her eyes. He was moving forward. It had been so hard for him, but he was doing it. She wanted to hug him, but she didn't want to force him, so she just nodded and opened her arms.

He stepped forward then back and roared again.

Not quite ready, she thought. That was okay. He was growing stronger inside himself and she couldn't be happier.

The next night she and Gavin spent another dinner with the children. The meal was calmer than the previous evening. Since Sam hadn't taken an afternoon nap, he was drooping throughout the meal.

Sara bathed Adelaide while Gavin bathed Sam. After the baths, the children quickly settled down.

She and Gavin left the nursery area and he captured his hand with hers. "Stay with me tonight," he said. "This may be our last chance for a while."

Sara's heart clenched at the need in his eyes. She couldn't imagine turning him down. "All right," she said, lacing her fingers through his and meeting his gaze.

He looked down and kissed her. His effect on her was so powerful that Sara almost forgot that someone could be watching.

"Let's take this into your suite or mine," she managed, and he led her into his living quarters.

"I can't stop wanting you. Can't stop wanting to be with you," he said as he stroked her hair.

"You're not the only one," she told him. "I want you, too."

Chapter Ten

The next morning, Sara and Gavin learned that the movers would be taking their belongings from the cottage to the new house. Gavin wanted to supervise the move, so he and Sara left the children in the capable hands of the palace nanny and quickly made the drive to the cottage.

Sara and Gavin walked through each of the rooms. "Looks like most of the clothing and toys are already gone," he mused.

"I've noticed that Princess Ericka is a woman of action. I should touch base with her about mattresses and upholstered furniture. Even though I know this place has been aired out, it still smells strongly of smoke," Sara said. Since her childhood experience with fire, the smell had often made her feel nauseated. "You don't mind if I get some fresh air, do you?"

Mr. Trevon walked beside her. "You know, for a long time, I couldn't put my finger on where I'd seen you before."

"I must have an everywoman face," she said and forced a smile.

"No. It's not that," he said. "I finally figured it out."

"You look like that princess who is a concert pianist," he said.

Sara's heart froze. She forced herself to take tiny breaths then laughed. "A princess," she echoed. "I'm flattered. And a concert pianist. I'm even more flattered."

"You really look like her," the man said. "And I heard you play the piano. You're very talented."

"And you're kind and generous," she managed, looking at him. "I'll cherish this moment of flattery for the rest of my life."

His face fell. "You're not a princess?"

She forced a chuckle. "Am I dressed like a princess?"

He paused, studying her, then rubbing his hand across his face. "Well, no."

"Exactly. I hate to disappoint you," she said.

"You just look so much like her," he said. "Beautiful. And you play the piano."

Sara smiled. "You are so kind. I'll remember this moment when I'm feeling down. Someone thought I was a princess."

He sighed. "Maybe you could make some money impersonating her."

Alarm flashed through her. "What an interesting possibility," she managed, horrified. "I may consider that in the future."

"Sara."

Sara turned at the sound of Gavin's voice just behind her. Her nerves tightened in fear. "I'm coming," she said and walked toward him.

"Are you okay?" Gavin asked, looking down at her in concern.

"I'm fine," she said. "Just needed a breath of air. Gavin, this is our neighbor Mr. Trevon," she said.

"Pleased to meet you," Mr. Trevon said. "I was just telling your children's nanny how much she resembled—"

"Oh my goodness, there are the moving trucks," she said, breaking into a sweat.

Gavin glanced toward the cottage. "You're right. We should go," he said. "Nice to meet you." He took Sara's hand and started walking back to the cottage.

He glanced down at her. "Your hand is freezing. Are you sure you're okay? You don't look like you're feeling so great."

At this point, she was more terrified by her encounter with the neighbor than anything, but she decided to put the focus on the fire. "Delayed reaction to the smell of smoke," she said. "It came out of nowhere."

He stopped and looked down at her. "Sorry."

Her heart stopped, then started again. "Thank you. I'm okay."

"Don't go in the house again. You can give the sniff test to the new house, too," he added.

She smiled. "I'll do that, but I suspect everything will be smoke-free thanks to Princess Ericka. The only issue may be the white tree."

"We'll get rid of it," he said.

"No," she said, shaking her head. "Sam wants the white tree, and it's already decorated. We might have a hard time finding another just like it."

"I thought he hated it," Gavin said as they waked into the driveway leading to the cottage.

"He changed his mind," she said.

"If it smells smoky, we'll keep the tree on the porch," he said.

"We'll figure it out," she said, and she felt herself turn into a melt at his concern.

Gavin supervised the movers. After the truck pulled away, he turned to her. "Would you like to stop somewhere to grab something to eat?"

Sara blinked in surprise. The simple invitation gave her a rush of pleasure. "That would be lovely."

"Any ideas?"

Sara nodded, remembering one unique spot where she and her sister had enjoyed a couple of meals. "There's a wonderful creperie. They serve both entrée and dessert crepes, and also sandwiches if you don't like crepes."

"Let's go," he said, and he helped her into the car.

Moments later, they sat at a booth in the small but famous crepe shop. Sara ordered a seafood crepe, Gavin ordered a sandwich and they agreed to share the Nutella crepe topped with strawberries and cream.

"How did you know about this place?" he asked.

"It's a local favorite," she said. "We were lucky to be seated so quickly. It's usually packed. Members of the royal family have even been known to come here on occasion."

"So it gets the royal stamp of approval," he said.

Sara smiled. "Something like that."

"How long have you been living in Chantaine?" he asked.

"A year," she said.

"And before?"

"I traveled a lot," she hedged. "I was ready for a change."

"I guess being a secret spy got to you," he said, humor playing at his lips.

She laughed and shook her head. "Not me. On another subject—"

"I notice you change the subject a lot when I ask you about your past," he said, opening his hand on the table in a gesture for her to put her hand in his.

Sara hesitated, but couldn't find the will to refuse him. The trouble was he wanted more than just to hold her hand. He wanted to know her secrets. In a different situation, she would trust him. But not now.

"You can't blame me for wanting to know more about you," he said.

"No," she said. "There's just a lot I can't talk about right now."

He nodded, then sighed. "Okay," he said. "About that other subject?"

Relief rushed through her. No more prodding. "Christmas gifts for the children," she said. "Have you made your list?"

He shot her a blank look. "I haven't even thought about it."

"Well, someone needs to do more than think about it," she said. "I don't think you'll be able to order much at this point, so the local toy shop will have to do. Your children are young, so hopefully they will be easy to please. Adelaide will be happy with a stuffed animal and an infant activity toy."

Gavin nodded. "I can't believe I didn't think about this."

"You've had a lot on your mind." She squeezed his hand.

"Well, we can take care of it this afternoon," he said with a determined expression on his face. "We'll go shopping after we eat."

"Today?" she echoed. "I thought we'd make a list."

"It's Saturday. We'll be moving during the next few days, and I'm still trying to push through this project. No time like the present," he said.

She couldn't help admiring his forceful attitude. Sara fell for him a little more. She could tell Gavin was struggling as a single dad, but he was determined to do everything he could to help his children feel secure and happy. "Your children are lucky to have you as their dad," she told him.

"Lucky?" he said in disbelief. "I forgot about Christmas gifts."

"You love them and you're not afraid to show it. That's a huge gift in itself," she said, thinking of her childhood. "Not every child has that."

"There's so much I want for them. I know I can't make their world perfect." Grief dragged at his brown eyes. "They've already suffered the loss of their mother, and I can't bring her back."

Sara felt a familiar sense of helplessness. With each passing day, she wanted to fix things for Gavin and his family, but she knew some things couldn't be fixed. "You're helping them to heal. I'm seeing glimmers of joy in Sam more and more often. When he drew with a green marker on both himself and Adelaide, I couldn't bring myself to scold him. He was acting like a normal three-year-old."

"When did this happen?" he asked.

"Oops. I guess I forgot to tell you. Sam decided that he was a frog and Adelaide was a turtle."

"I wish I'd seen that," he said.

"I would imagine it could happen again. Give him free use of markers, and send him in to amuse Adelaide," she said.

Gavin chuckled. "Bet you put the markers away."

"Let's just say use of the markers will now require supervision. I was just relieved the ink wasn't waterproof," she said.

"Sam is growing more relaxed with you," Gavin said. "We may have to find a way to keep you around."

Sara felt her heart dip at the expression in his eyes. She wasn't exactly sure what he was suggesting. Keep her? For how long? She should remind him that this was a temporary assignment. She should remind herself that her relationship with all of them was temporary.

The waiter delivered their food, saving her from responding aloud. But inside, her voice was screaming warnings. Sara chose to focus on her seafood crepe and the gorgeous single dad sitting across from her. While she could.

Gavin almost couldn't believe how happy he felt Christmas shopping for the kids with Sara. His wife had shooed him away when he'd tried to join her for the task. He disliked shopping as much as the next man, but trying to get it done in two hours brought out his competitive spirit. The shopping cart almost full, he watched Sara frowning in concentration as she studied a book.

"What's the problem?" he asked.

"Nothing," she said. "I just want to make sure this is age appropriate. This book is about frogs, but it may be a bit advanced for Sam."

Gavin snagged the book from her hands and tossed it into the cart. "He'll grow into it. Besides, if he's into frogs then he'll concentrate more so he can learn more. We're all like that as kids. I bet you were, too. Maybe with the piano."

Sara hesitated, then nodded. "Yes, you're right. And what about you?" she asked.

"Legos, math and my hamster. Don't laugh," he said when she bit her lip in amusement. "That was the only pet I was allowed to have besides a goldfish. My mom had allergies."

"And you wanted a dog," she said. "A big dog."

"Yes. Still waiting on that. My wife didn't want a pet. Since we're only in Chantaine for a while, this isn't the time to get one."

"Unless it's a frog," she said.

"Only if it comes with batteries," he said. "Can you imagine trying to get a frog past Customs?"

"You have a point. But if you were staying in Chantaine, I'd be getting you a puppy for Christmas," she said. "If you've been wanting one your whole life, then I'd say you're overdue."

In her voice he heard a hint of indignation on his behalf, and it filled up one of the cracks of pain he'd tried to ignore for so long. She was the most generous woman he'd ever met. "I appreciate the thought more than you know. We'd better hit the Lego aisle if we're going to get out of here in fifteen minutes."

Sara checked her watch. "Right-o," she said. "It wouldn't be fair not to give Binnie a break soon. I wonder if we should call to check on the children."

"Stay focused," he said even as he cherished her devotion to his children. "The palace staff have my number and they have yours."

"True," she said.

They finished shopping, and Sara insisted on getting wrapping paper and supplies. As Gavin pulled into a parking space at the palace, he felt a twinge of regret that the day was over. He realized how much he wanted his own time with Sara. He wanted the opportunity to watch her emotions play out on her face. He wanted to tease her and make her laugh. And always, always, he wanted to make love to her.

Gavin had avoided thinking about his own needs for so long that his feelings caught him off guard. "Just one more thing..." He slid his hand behind her neck to draw her closer to him. "Thanks," he said against her lips, then kissed her.

When he pulled back, she looked at him in surprise. "For what?"

"Life's been a grind for a while now. Today was fun," he said.

She met his gaze and nodded. "It was for me, too." She glanced from side to side, then pressed her mouth against his. He immediately felt a rush of heat and want. That little demonstration of her desire for him got under his skin.

He deepened the kiss and savored the taste of her,

her quick and passionate response. Wanting more, he pulled her across the center console and slid his hands beneath her blouse. He craved the sensation of feeling her bare skin.

She squeezed his shoulders and tilted her head, inviting him to take her further. He slid his hands over her breasts and found her nipples hard with arousal. Gavin was hard, too. He wanted to feel her moistness closing around him. He wanted to strip off her jeans and underwear and take her right there.

A car horn beeped, barely permeating his consciousness. Gavin slid his tongue over hers, wanting her naked. Wanting her to be his.

The car horn beeped again.

"What the—" Gavin said, looking out the foggy back windows. He caught sight of a vehicle with flashing lights.

A man knocked on the tinted window and Gavin lowered it. "Problem?" Gavin asked.

"Just wanted to make sure you were okay," the palace guard said. "We check the parking lot every fifteen minutes."

Gavin nodded, putting his hand over Sara's. "We're okay. We were just talking about Christmas gifts for my children."

The guard nodded. "I feel your pain. I have one of my own. Let me know if you need any help."

Gavin pushed the button to lift his window and took a deep breath. He needed to get his libido under control.

"Christmas gifts?" Sara said. "We were nearly having sex in the palace parking lot."

"What else was I going to say? I want to make love to the nanny of my children so stop interrupting?"

Sara pushed her hair from her head and looked away, sighing. "I do wonder how far we would have gone if we hadn't been interrupted."

"I can tell you," Gavin said, sliding his hand behind the nape of her neck. "All the way."

"Don't you dare get started," she said with a scowl, fanning her face. "You are too irresistible for my own good."

Sara wasn't quite sure how she got through the evening. Apparently the move would take place sometime tomorrow, although the family wouldn't have to leave the palace immediately.

Sara, however, suspected the Sinclair family needed to get settled into their new space as soon as possible. She could do nothing about it tonight, though, because clothing and stuffed animals and toys were being cleaned. The advantage of having the palace on your side.

She and Gavin spent time with the children, then collapsed in the sitting area of his bedroom suite. "How did we function before the palace nanny?"

"I'm not sure I always functioned all that well," she admitted, leaning back to close her eyes for just a moment.

"Yes you have," he said. "Little children require a lot of attention, supervision and care."

"And frozen washcloths for teething pain," she added, still keeping her eyes closed. Her eyelids felt as if ten pound weights were resting on them. "Don't forget that."

A few seconds passed. "That's right. You also reminded me about buying Christmas gifts."

Sara nodded and sighed. She heard Gavin say something else, but didn't compute his words. She shifted slightly in her chair and the room faded away.

Moments later, she felt something shift beneath her. Sara opened her eyes and found herself in Gavin's arms. "What—"

"I was talking. You were snoring," he said. "I'm putting you to bed." Carrying her from his room to hers, he set her down on her bed, then pulled off her shoes "I'd offer to take off your clothes, but then I'd want to keep you awake."

Despite her weariness, his sexy smile made her heart turn over. "I can't remember feeling this tired. I apologize," she said.

"No apologies," he said. "Sleep." He bent down and dropped a kiss on her lips. "Good night, beautiful."

Sara knew she should get up and change into her nightgown, but the mattress felt so good and despite the fact that she knew she looked worn-out and messy, she felt more beautiful than she could ever remember.

When she awakened in the morning, her mouth felt grimy and her eyes were gritty. She crawled out of bed, stripped off her clothes and turned on the shower. Standing under the spray, she turned her face up to the warm water and let it flow over her. It felt so good. She sudsed up, then rinsed and spent an extra couple of minutes absorbing the water therapy. She finally, reluctantly, turned off the water and left the shower. Drying off, she scrubbed her hair with a towel, then pulled her hair into a bun that would take hours to air dry.

Bother, she thought. This day was going to be extremely busy. She added some lip gloss and some tinted moisturizer that would probably slide off within two hours, but she felt compelled to make an effort. Pulling on a pair of jeans and a long-sleeve T-shirt, she then put on her tennis shoes.

Sara mentally girded herself. She was ready for the marathon that would take place today. At the same time she was giving herself the pep talk, a knock sounded at the door. She opened it to a staff member carrying a tray with breakfast.

"You are a gift from the heavens," she said.

The young man's mouth twitched in humor as he set the tray down on a table. "You're welcome, Your Highness."

Sara dropped the stainless-steel cover she'd just lifted from the tray and gaped at him. "You don't need to address me that way," she said. "But thank you again," she said.

"As you wish, ma'am," he said. "I was just trying to be respectful of your position. Have I offended you?"

"No," she said. "I just think you may be mistaken. I'm not a Your Highness or a ma'am."

"Yes, ma—" He broke off. "Yes," he said and left the room.

Sara glanced at the food. Her appetite had fled. She knew that secrets could spread quickly among staff. She wondered who had heard that she was royalty, and she prayed it wouldn't spread outside the castle.

Despite her lack of appetite, she knew she should eat

something, so she forced herself to eat a few bites of an omelet and toast. Her mind was whirling. She needed to talk to someone in the royal family, but she wasn't sure who could provide her with the truth.

Chapter Eleven

Sara walked out of her bedroom and immediately ran into Gavin in the hallway.

"How'd you sleep, princess?" he asked with a grin.

Sara flinched even though she knew he was just addressing her as a princess out of affection. Her interaction with the server had put her on edge.

"Not so well, I guess," Gavin said.

"I'm fine," she said. "I'm great."

"Keep saying it and you'll believe it," he said as he slid his arm around her. "Take a deep breath. We're just starting."

"I know," she said. "There's so much we need to do."

"It's okay if all of it doesn't get done right away," Gavin said.

She looked at him in disbelief. "Says the perfectionist project engineer determined to keep his project on schedule."

"Touché," he said.

Sara finally took that deep breath. "Forgive me. I was impolite. We'll just do the best we can."

"And that will be more than enough," he said. "If we had wineglasses, we would toast. Instead," he said, and lowered his mouth to hers, "we'll kiss."

Sara kissed him, then drew back. "How are we going to keep our relationship secret if we keep kissing in public?"

"Do we really need to keep it secret?" he asked and took her hand in his.

Sara paused. "We do right now," she said.

He pulled his hand away from hers. "As you wish."

It's not what I wish, she wanted to say. It's what's necessary. Instead she said, "Thank you."

She joined Gavin in his car and they followed Princess Ericka, her husband and their toddler son to the new house. The drive was mostly quiet—Sara hated the tension between her and Gavin, but she didn't feel she could do anything about it.

Sara watched Ericka's car pull into the driveway of a chalet much larger than the cottage where the family had previously lived.

"Nice digs," Gavin muttered as he pulled into the driveway.

"I agree," she said. "I wonder what the interior looks like."

"We'll find out soon," he said. He got out of the car and rounded it to help her from her seat, but she was already walking toward the chalet.

Princess Ericka turned toward them with a huge smile on her face. "Welcome to your new home."

Sara shook her head. "I don't know what to say. It's beautiful."

"It wasn't available when you first arrived, Mr. Sinclair, but we're happy to offer this residence for the rest of your contract."

"It's beautiful," Sara said.

"How's the electrical?" Gavin asked.

Ericka's husband stepped forward and extended his hand to Gavin. "Hi, I'm Treat. The electrical system is the best in Chantaine. We apologize for the trauma you experienced at the cottage, and we're working to bring all the electrical work up to code. I'm with you on the electrical situation. Unfortunately, this is an island with a lot of older homes, and many owners haven't bothered to update. We're working to make it a requirement. The fire department concluded its investigation on your previous residence. It was a result of faulty wiring in the laundry room."

"That's good to know. I hope you're requiring all homes to have smoke alarms," he said as they all stepped into the house.

"This has already been voted into law. Chantaine residents are known for their independence, so it may take a few citations for some people to realize we mean business."

"Oh, look, "Sara said, glancing into the spacious den. "The white tree is already up. Sam will be so happy."

"How's the smell?" Gavin asked.

Sara gave it a sniff. "No smoke."

"We aired it out and treated it, but you may need to give it a spray of freshener every now and then," Ericka said.

"Thanks," Gavin said. "Sara had a bad experience

with a house fire when she was a child, so the smell of smoke isn't a favorite."

"Of course not," Ericka said, her face softening in concern. "I'm sorry to hear that."

Feeling self-conscious, Sara shrugged. "I'm quite fine. I don't know how to thank you for all you've done. The house is beautiful."

"I'm glad you like it," Ericka said as she led the way down the hall. "There are four bedrooms. The nursery and Sam's room are connected through a bathroom, and Sara will have her own bath in the back. The master is to your right."

Leo raced down the hallway and squealed with joy. "Mama. Cookies."

Ericka bent down to her child. "It's not time for cookies." She glanced at Sara and Gavin and smiled. "He's full of energy these days. It seems like he went from crawling to running." She turned back to the tot. "Go see Daddy. We won't be staying much longer."

"Daddy?" he echoed.

Ericka nodded and watched her son zoom down the hallway. "It's always exciting when he says a word. The surgery has made such a difference for him."

"I noticed the device behind his ear," Gavin said.

"Yes. It's a special transmitter. It's not a cure for his hearing disability, and we're still working on sign language, but it's thrilling to see him making progress like other children."

"He certainly seems healthy and robust to me," Sara said.

"Yes, he is," Ericka said. "We use the term *wild child* every now and then." She gave a light laugh. "But back to the house. The clothing, toys and linens have been cleaned. As you can see, we're using different furniture. Some things have been put away, but there are boxes of your belongings in each room."

"You're a miracle worker," Sara said.

"Not at all," Ericka demurred. "All of you have been through a difficult time. We just want to make things a little easier. Stefan has been quite adamant that he wants Mr. Sinclair's distractions kept to a minimum. He's eager for the completion of the project you're doing for Chantaine."

"I got that impression," Gavin said in a dry tone.

"Stefan can be quite the taskmaster. His intentions are good, but all of us have learned that we have to push back on occasion. If you don't have any other questions, I'll go rescue my husband from our little cookie monster and be on our way."

"I'd like to try to get Sam's room as ready as possible," Sara said. "He's been through a lot of changes."

"Yes, he has. If you need to stay at the palace another night, that's totally fine," Ericka said. "Oh, and before I forget, you're all invited to the palace Christmas-tree lighting this week. If you need anything at all, I'm just a phone call away."

"Thank you again," Gavin said.

The princess and her family left, and Sara and Gavin immediately went to Sam's room. "I want to unpack his toys and put some pictures on the wall. Speaking of pictures, we need to put the photo of his mother on the dresser. I'm sure you have other photos of Sam and Adelaide," she said.

"I've got tons on my laptop and my phone."

"I think it would be a good idea to put some copies

of other photos on his dresser. It might be comforting to him. I'd like to put some photos in Adelaide's room, too"

"Good idea," he said as he took her hand. "You're always thinking of new ways to help them."

She bit her lip at the intent expression on his face. "It's my job," she said and smiled.

"Nothing more? You're not at all attached?"

"Of course I am. How could I not love your children?" she said, trying not to think about how she was going to feel when her job was done. There was no way she could emotionally distance herself from the family. *Don't think about the future*, she told herself. She had to focus on the task in front of her. "I hope there's a shop open on Sunday where we can get photos printed," she said.

"I have a color printer if I can find it," he said.

"Perfect," she said. "You look for it and I'll unpack some boxes."

"Will do," he said, and they each got to work.

Gavin drove to a shop and watched Sara meticulously choose several frames for the photos she wanted to display in Sam's room. He was pretty pleased with himself that he'd printed off a picture of a frog he'd found on the internet. Sara had been, too.

"This frog photo is fabulous," she told Gavin. "I know Sam is going to love it."

Her praise was like cool soothing water in the pained cracks of his heart. His wife had criticized him far more than she'd acknowledged his efforts. Sara made him feel as if he could fly. She made him think he wasn't such a bad father after all.

"This is going to be wonderful," Sara said. "You did a great job."

"I just printed off a few photos," he said. "That's nothing."

"It's not nothing," she protested. "Those photos are going to make an impact on Sam every day. You're a wonderful father. Sam is so lucky to have you."

Something inside him expanded. As after an exercise he hadn't done often enough, he felt a little sore but invigorated at the same time. "Lucky?"

"Yes, lucky," she said, smiling as she looked at the photos. "These are wonderful," she said. "They will be healing for both Sam and Adelaide. Let's go back to hang them. Do you want to wait till tomorrow to move?"

The excitement in her voice lifted his spirits. He shook his head. "No, I think we need to get settled for however long we'll be in Chantaine. Adelaide may be okay, but I think all the changes affect Sam."

"That sounds wise," Sara said.

He stared at her for a long moment. Sara had helped the children turn a corner. She was helping to lift the whole family out of the mire of their grief.

He knew his stint in Chantaine wouldn't last forever, but Sara was good medicine for his family. He wanted to find a way to keep her around for longer than his time in Chantaine. He wanted to keep her around for a long time. He was determined to find a way.

The family made the big move that evening. The children seemed delighted with their new digs. "How long will we be here?" Sam asked.

"Until we go back to the States," Gavin said.

"I wanna stay here," Sam said. "Can we stay here?"

"For a while," Gavin said as he met Sara's gaze.

"Can we play duck, duck, goose?" Sam asked.

Gavin groaned.

"Yes, we can," Sara said, shooting a dark glance at Gavin. "Everyone gets tired after playing duck, duck, goose."

Gavin chuckled. "As you say," he said, and he joined the game.

An hour later, after too many games of duck, duck, goose, a round of video games and several books read aloud, Gavin and Sara collapsed on the sofa. Sara leaned her head back. "Wow, that was a lot. I hope they sleep well," she said.

"Me, too," Gavin said. "How do they have so much energy?"

"They didn't unpack and hang photos," she reminded him, her eyes still closed.

"True," he said. "Thanks for all you did today. I think Sam is coming around."

"I hope so," she said. "I just want him to heal and be happy. Maybe I'm asking too much."

"I'm asking for the same thing," he said. "Speaking of asking. What does Sara want for Christmas?"

Sara chuckled. "Oh, my goodness. I can't think of a thing, except maybe the opportunity to sleep for at least twenty-four hours."

Gavin heard the weariness in her voice and wanted to make it up to her. "I'll see what I can do about that."

She laughed again. "I was joking," she said. "I'm fine."

Gavin nodded, but his brain was turning. He would find a way for Sara to have her break, and maybe he would take a break with her.

* * *

Over the next two days, Sara divided her time between wrapping gifts for the children and helping them get settled into the house. She missed the piano but tried not to think about it. She had plenty else to do, and there really wasn't a good place for it in this house.

Ericka had invited Tabitha and herself for a Christmas Tea with the Devereaux women, and she'd been considerate enough to provide a sitter for Sam and Adelaide. How could she turn the Devereaux family down?

Truthfully, she couldn't. After giving Tabitha a little nudge, her sister agreed to attend. Sara worried about Tabitha. Her sister didn't seem herself.

Sara drove to the palace for brunch, pulled into the parking lot and was immediately admitted into the building. A wave of nostalgia flowed over her as she remembered walking into the tumbledown palace from her childhood with no ID. The guards had known her by her face and her voice. She'd always tried to be polite and gracious.

After the attacks against her family, she wondered how successful she'd been at conveying her gratitude. Walking into the one of the smaller palace dining rooms, she noticed that many of the royal family were already in attendance. Her sister, Tabitha, however, was nowhere in sight.

Ericka glanced up. "There you are," she said as she stood. "I'm so glad you came. And where is your sister?"

"She's driving herself," Sara said. "I'm sure she'll be here soon. Merry Christmas."

"Merry Christmas to you." Ericka embraced Sara. "I don't need to introduce you, but I'll refresh your memory just in case. Eve's on the other side of the table. Bridget sits to the left of her. Pippa, enormously pregnant, sits to the right. I hope Pippa makes it through tea," Ericka said in a low voice."

Sara chuckled. "She looks fine to me."

"Well, let's get a spot of tea. Hopefully Tabitha will arrive soon," she said.

"Hopefully," Sara muttered to herself.

Eve, the Texan wife of the ruling prince Stefan, glanced up from her conversation with Pippa. "Welcome, welcome," she said, rising from her chair and walking around the table to give Sara a big hug. "How are you surviving? I bet this has felt like forever for you."

"It has gone on longer than I anticipated, but I'm very grateful for the safety your family has extended to my sister and me," she said. "I think the hardest part has been not getting any news about Alex."

"Yes, I understand. I lost track of my brother for years. It was such a gift when Stefan located him again. I'll see what I can do to remind him. In the meantime, I'm hearing that the Sinclairs are thrilled with your service to their family. You got up to speed in record time."

"Yes, she has," Ericka said. "And this hasn't been the easiest assignment with the grief the family has been suffering." She made a sympathetic tsking sound.

"I think they're all making progress, but it's challenging balancing their grief with the joy of Christmas. You can't just skip Christmas when you have children," Sara said.

"Of course not," Bridget said from her place at the table. "And speaking of Christmas, I think you and the

Kincaids should join us for Christmas dinner. Tell Mr. Sinclair I insist."

"That sounds lovely—"

Tabitha burst into the room. "Sorry, I'm late," she said. "I had to pull a few extra hours at the restaurant. At least no one is trying to kidnap me. So these are commoner concerns," she said with a saucy grin that looked a little forced to Sara.

The Devereaux women chuckled in unison and Sara suspected they were completely charmed.

"Oh, you poor thing," Bridget said. "I hate it that you have to work so hard."

"It could be worse," Tabitha said. "I could have Sara's job. Heaven help the children under my care."

The whole group of women giggled. Except Sara.

Something about Tabitha's expression seemed a bit brittle. A bit off. She frowned, wondering what was really wrong.

Tabitha glanced at her. "Oh, no. Have I offended you?"

"Not at all," Sara said. "I feel as if I'm doing something important with the Sinclair family. I just want you to be well."

Silence followed.

Tabitha chuckled. "You know me. I'm always better than well."

But Sara suspected something about Tabitha was wrong. She just wasn't sure how to learn what exactly that was.

Sara enjoyed the tea. It had been a while since she'd taken a formal tea, so it was a pleasure. At the same time, she couldn't stop noticing that Tabitha just didn't seem right. Tabitha ate very little and excused herself to go to the restroom. Her sister's face looked a bit gaunt.

Sara prayed Tabitha wasn't truly ill. She followed her to the restroom during her second trip. "Tabitha," she said.

Tabitha glanced at her over her shoulder. "Sorry. Can't stop. I think I have food poisoning," she said before she vanished into the bathroom and apparently spilled her stomach.

Sara waited outside the restroom for her sister. When Tabitha walked outside, Sara immediately confronted her. "I'm afraid there's something wrong with you. You've been ill for too long," she said.

Tabitha waved her concerns away. "I'm not ill. I just have a little nausea. It will pass soon. I'm betting it will be gone by next weekend."

"Hmm," Sara said. "I think you should go to the doctor. In fact, I insist."

"Insist?" Tabitha echoed. "Have you ever known me to respond to demands?"

Sara sighed. "Can you respond to loving concern?"

Tabitha also sighed. "Well, I suppose that's different."

"I just want you to be okay. Can you blame me? You and I may be all we have left. Alexander may be gone to us."

"I don't believe he's gone," Tabitha said. "In fact, when we find out where he's been, I suspect we'll be irritated, if not angry with him."

"Really?" Sara said more than asked, amazed by Tabitha's prediction.

"Yes, really," Tabitha said. "We're all worked up,

worried and growing older by the minute and I'll bet we'll find that Alex is perfectly fine and safe."

"I wish I shared your optimism," Sara said.

During the rest of the tea, Tabitha was her charming, amusing self, but Sara just knew something was going on with her sister. She wasn't sure what it was, but she suspected it was important.

"Sara and Tabitha—" Bridget cleared her throat. "Jane," she corrected herself. "You just don't seem like a Jane. No matter. I want to remind you that you're invited to my house for Christmas dinner. Don't forget," Bridget said. "Don't refuse me."

Tabitha laughed. "I like your spirit. It matches mine. That said, don't feel bad if I can't come. My restaurant is serving a special meal on Christmas Day."

All of the Devereaux women frowned in disapproval. "Well, I don't like that," Pippa said.

"Neither do I," Bridget said.

"Nor I," said Eve.

Tabitha smiled. "It's not that bad. I won't be digging ditches. If I have one Christmas wish, it's that Alex will be found soon."

Ericka exchanged a glance with Eve. "Perhaps we can work on that Christmas wish, Eve," Ericka said.

"I think it's time to talk with Stefan. This has gone on too long," Eve said.

Bridget chuckled. "Good luck, Stefan," she said. "Now, speaking of Christmas, have you completed all of your shopping? And where are you hiding your gifts? One of my boys has already located a gift intended for my daughter."

"Oh, dear," Pippa said. "Thank goodness Amelie isn't quite that curious yet."

"You can always hide them at the palace," Eve offered.

"We're putting Sam's at the top of my closet. He's not much of a climber. At the moment," she added. "So I'm hoping they'll be safe from his discovery. I would like to give Sam an opportunity to decorate cookies, but I'm not much of a cook. I haven't ever made cookies."

"That's easy," Bridget said. "There are these rolls of cookie dough you can buy at the food market. You just slice up the dough, bake them and the children can add canned frosting and sprinkles. They love it."

"I'm afraid it's something most of us have in common. I never really had to cook for myself," Pippa said.

"Well, I did," Eve said, "But I wasn't raised as a royal. I agree with Bridget on the refrigerator cookies. They're easy and take care of the job."

"Thanks for the hint," Sara said, glad to know she wasn't the only one who had been raised without some real-life skills.

The Devereaux women continued to discuss their children and husbands and plans for Christmas. After the tea concluded, Sara followed her sister to her apartment.

"Forgive the untidiness," Tabitha said, waving a hand toward a chair full of laundry. "I haven't felt much like cleaning lately. I finally got around to doing some laundry."

"I can help you fold," Sara said. "But I am starting to get worried about you. You're just so pale, and I noticed you didn't eat much at the palace tea at all."

Tabitha made a face. "I wasn't in the mood for sweets.

Well, I wasn't in the mood for much of anything. But stop fussing. This can't last forever. I'm sure it's just a bug that's hanging on."

"I think it's time for you to see a doctor. I insist," she said.

Tabitha's eyes widened. "We've already discussed this."

"It's for your own good," Sara said. "Sit down and let me fix some tea."

Sara went to the adjoining kitchen and fixed two cups, then returned to the den. Tabitha was leaning back against the sofa with her eyes closed.

"Are you asleep?" Sara asked.

Her sister opened her eyes and yawned. "Not yet. This must be part of the little bug I have."

"All the more reason for you to go to the doctor. Promise me you will," Sara said.

"Let me give it a few more days," Tabitha said. "I don't want to have to make up a new history for the doctor."

"You can just tell him the truth about your health. That shouldn't be too hard. And I want you to call tomorrow. You may not be able to get an appointment right away," Sara insisted. "If you don't do it, then I will."

Tabitha lifted her hand. "Okay, okay. I'll make an appointment tomorrow, but I'm expecting to heal miraculously overnight."

Sara let out a little breath. Part of her concern for her sister was selfish. With Alex missing, her sister was the only member of her family she knew was still alive. Despite the fact that Sara and Tabitha were as different as night and day, she'd always adored her sister and spoiled her whenever she'd gotten the opportunity.

She took a sip of tea, then put down the cup. "We haven't had enough time together and I've really been missing you."

"I know what you mean," Tabitha said, her expression turning serious. "When I heard about the fire I was so upset. I couldn't eat or sleep even after you called me. I kept thinking about that terrible fire in the palace when they'd gotten everyone out except you."

Sara hugged her sister. "That was a frightening time for all of us."

"But it was worse for you, and your injuries were worse," Tabitha said, shuddering at the memory.

Sara lifted her palms and looked at them. "Everything still works. I guess I'm lucky."

"I know you told me you didn't panic when the smoke alarm went off, but you had to have some kind of reaction."

Feeling a twinge of restlessness, Sara went to the chair filled with clothes and began to fold them. "The sound of the alarm was terrible and the smell of smoke took me back for a few seconds, but then I knew I had to get the children out of the house. I was more concerned about getting them to safety than anything. My fingers did shake when I called emergency. After the fire truck came and Gavin arrived, I felt relieved. Gavin hugged all of us."

"Oh, he did, did he? And have you and he progressed in the romantic department?" her sister prodded.

Sara really didn't want to discuss her relationship with Gavin. It was so complicated. "It doesn't really matter," she said. "It's all temporary. Our situation here—" She broke off. "It's just beginning to feel like I woke up one day with a different identity. Like I got kidnapped to be in the circus. I know we're safer here than we would be in Sergenia and I'm grateful to the Devereaux family for taking us in when no one else appeared willing. But—"

"But?" Tabitha prompted.

"But I want to find Alex and I want to stop lying about who I am. I want you and me to get on with our lives. Whatever that may mean."

Chapter Twelve

Sara arrived at the new house late that night. She'd helped Tabitha with laundry and cleaning and even heated a can of soup without burning it—a huge accomplishment. She stayed with her sister until Tabitha fell asleep on the couch for the second time. Then Sara urged her sister to get ready for bed.

Walking into the house, she noticed the sound of soft jazz music and subdued lighting in the den. Gavin appeared from the hallway with two glasses of white wine. "Ready to relax?" he asked.

She smiled at the sight of LED candles lit throughout the room. "I'm surprised. I thought you might have been overwhelmed with the children after the sitter left."

"Binnie showed up, and I only managed the evening."

Sara stepped toward him and accepted the glass of wine. She took a sip and allowed the cool liquid to slide down her throat. "Well, it appears you've done a good job if both children are in bed."

Gavin took her hand and led her to the sofa. "I'm not sure how she does it, but I think the palace nanny wears them out."

Sara took another sip of her wine. "I must talk to her and learn her secret," she said.

He gave a short chuckle. "You're doing pretty well on your own. How was the tea and the rest of your day?"

"The palace was so generous to include me and—" she broke off when she almost mentioned Tabitha "—another non-Devereaux. It was lovely. They were so welcoming and I received a tip for baking cookies for the children to decorate. I plan to do that soon with Sam and Adelaide."

"And afterward?" he asked, drinking from his own glass of wine.

"There wasn't much time afterward," she hedged. "I did a bit of window shopping and ran into a friend I met when I first moved to Chantaine."

He skimmed his fingertips over the inside of wrist. "Are you tired?"

She nodded. "But not as tired as I have been," she said. "What about you?"

"It's good to know I'll be sleeping in the same bed I'm going to sleep in for the next several weeks."

"I think you're right," she said.

"Otherwise, it's camping," he said.

Sara thought about all the times she'd spent only one or two nights in a country when she'd been on a concert tour. "Or work," she said.

"Sounds like you've been there," he said. "Not that you'll tell me much more."

She smiled. "Correct on both counts."

He gave a faux put-upon sigh. "Okay," he said. "I have an early Christmas gift for you. It's not perfect, but I'm hoping it will make the transition a little easier."

"A gift?" she said, delighted. "What on earth did you get me? I need nothing."

"Need and want merge every now and then," he said, setting down his glass of wine on the coffee table and rising.

Curious, Sara watched him as he left the room, then quickly reentered. "An electric piano," he said, carrying the instrument into the room. "It's not as good as a real piano, but maybe this will help you get by."

Sara was so moved she could barely speak. "I don't know what to say," she said, her eyes filling with tears. "I can't remember when someone did something this thoughtful for me."

"Hmm," he said in a short husky tone. "Then maybe you've been hanging around the wrong people."

Sara turned the electric piano volume on low and played a scale then a short song. She looked up at Gavin. "This is going to be wonderful for both me and the children. I can see both of them wanting to play with it. And when I say play, I mean learn. I don't know how to thank you," she said, rising from the piano and throwing herself into his arms.

"That's a damn good start," Gavin said, holding her against him. "I just want you to be happy. I just want you to stay with us."

That last sentence frightened her. Sara knew she couldn't stay with the Sinclairs forever. She had an assignment and would do her very best to fulfill it, but the time would come when she and the Sinclairs would have to say goodbye.

Pain twisted through her at the thought.

What should she say? What could she say?

Sara was determined to focus on this special moment instead of her fears for the future. "Gavin, I don't know what to say. No one has given me a more meaningful gift. In my entire life." She pressed her mouth against his.

"You're important to my children," Gavin said. "You're important to me."

"Oh, Gavin," she said.

He pressed his finger against her lips. "Let me make love to you," he said.

Sara stared into his passion-filled eyes and couldn't imagine rejecting him. "Yes," she whispered, and he led her down the hall to his room.

The way he undressed her made her feel as if she were a gift he was opening. He kissed her forehead and cheek with such tenderness. He touched her with an emotion deeper than the rush and power of passion.

She stared into his precious eyes and felt such a longing in her soul. She didn't want to be with him just tonight. She wanted to be with him every night. For the rest of her life.

Oh, no. She'd gone and done it.

She'd fallen in love with Gavin Sinclair.

The next morning, Sara took Sam for his last day of preschool before the Christmas break. He'd missed a day last week and seemed more excited than usual. She smiled at him as she drove toward the preschool.

"You seem happy to go to school today," she said.

He nodded. "I'm gonna get a treat," he said, rubbing his tummy.

She laughed. "How do you know that?"

"Cuz I saw you put a piece of chocolate in my snack bag," he said.

"Well, aren't you the observant one?" she said. "We're going to be doing some fun things during the next few days. We're going to a tree lighting at the palace tomorrow and we're also going to decorate Christmas cookies."

"Cookies," he said, glowing with excitement. "I love cookies."

"We'll be decorating them before we eat them, and we'll want to share some with your father."

"Daddy likes cookies, too," Sam said.

Sara felt a secret little joy at the knowledge that Sam was starting to smile more often. She knew he would always miss his mother, but she hoped he was starting to have some happiness, too.

After she dropped him off at preschool, Sara ran errands with Adelaide in tow. Thank goodness the cook and housekeeper was coming this afternoon. There wasn't much food in the house. She went to the food market and picked up a few necessities that they always seemed to need and use, along with slice-and-bake cookies and colored sugars and frosting for decorating.

Chuckling to herself, she realized she might be just as excited as Sam about decorating the cookies. It had been a long time since she'd done such a thing. She laid Adelaide down for an abbreviated nap, put the groceries away and took advantage of the quiet time to wrap a few packages.

Before she knew it, it was time to pick up Sam. Back

in the car she went with Adelaide. Poor baby, she'd had to awaken her from her nap. A teacher escorted Sam to the car as Sara took her turn in the pickup line. The woman helped Sam into the car and Sara helped strap him into his safety seat.

"I just wanted you to know that Sam had a very good day today. He played well with the other children and really seemed to enjoy himself," she said.

"I'm glad to hear that," Sara said, smiling at Sam in approval. "Good for you."

"We had cookies and we played an elf game," he said. "And we made a mistletoe. I got one to bring home."

"It sounds wonderful," Sara said. She turned to the teacher. "Thank you so much. I'll pass along the good news to Sam's father. He'll be very pleased."

"We're happy with his progress. Merry Christmas to all of you," she said.

"Merry Christmas," Sara said, and then she drove them home.

As soon as they entered the house, Sam pulled a sprig of mistletoe with red and green ribbon from his bag. "We need to hang this up high. People are supposed to kiss each other when they stand under it."

"Oh, my goodness. It sounds magical," she said. "Let me put Adelaide on her blanket in the den. Where do you think we should hang it?"

Sara placed Adelaide on her blanket and kept one eye on her as Sam bounced with excitement in the hallway.

"Up there," he said, pointing to the doorway entrance to the den. "Here," he said, pushing the mistletoe and a bag with an adhesive strip into her hands.

"I think I'm going to need a chair for this," she said

and got one from the dining area. "How about you hold the chair while I put up the mistletoe?"

Sam nodded and gripped the chair with his small hands.

Sara secured the mistletoe with the adhesive strip, then stepped down. "There we are. It looks good. You did a great job, Sam," she said and bent down to squeeze his shoulder.

"Since you're standing under the mistletoe, somebody's supposed to kiss you," he said solemnly.

"Oh, well, who can do that?" she asked.

"I can," he said and gave her the quickest, sweetest little kiss on her cheek.

Stunned, Sara felt as if her heart would burst into a million pieces of joy. Tears filled her eyes and she blinked them back. "Thank you very much, Sam." She pulled him into her arms and hugged him for a moment, and he squeezed her back.

"Can we have lunch now?" he asked.

"Of course," she managed, breathlessly laughing at the irony. She felt as if she and Sam had just experienced a monumental moment. She'd been waiting and hoping for him to start accepting affection. Now he could and she was so excited she was trembling. Sam, however, was over it and ready for the next thing. Lunch.

The following day, all the palace employees and contractors were dismissed after lunch. Despite the fire at the cottage and the ensuing uproar, Gavin had solved the glitch that was holding back progress on the project and great strides had been made in the past couple of days. As he drove home, Gavin looked forward to spending the rest of the day with Sara and the kids. Just remembering how her body had felt against his last night aroused him. He couldn't seem to get enough of her, and it wasn't just the sex. Something about her just felt as if she fed his soul.

He rolled his eyes at the romantic notion, but couldn't deny the truth. The more time he spent with Sara, the more he included her in his picture of the future, and the kids were growing attached to her, too. He thought the attachment was reciprocal, but whenever he mentioned the future, she was vague or changed the subject.

He wished she would trust him with her secrets, but it was almost as if someone had given her a gag order. That part of her situation frustrated the hell out of him, and it was all he could do not to push her for more information. Although he had no idea what her secrets were, except for her missing brother, he liked to think he might be able to help her with her problems. He just needed more information.

Pulling into the driveway of the new house, he cut the engine and got out. As soon as he opened the door, he was greeted by the scent of freshly baked cookies. He heard the voices of Sam and Sara coming from the kitchen.

"Good job, Sam. I like what you did with the red, green and blue sugars on that cookie," Sara said.

"Can we draw a frog on one of the cookies?" Sam asked.

Silence followed and he couldn't help feeling a spurt of amusement. He could just imagine Sara's expression of dismay.

"We certainly can try. We've got green frosting gel and green sprinkles," she said.

Gavin rounded the corner and found Sara and Sam

at the table while Adelaide sat in her high chair with white frosting and red sugar on her face and fingers. She was playing in a small dab of frosting on her tray.

"I can't wait to see that frog cookie," Gavin said, and both Sara and Sam looked up at him.

"I'll just bet you can't," Sara retorted with a smile.

Sam bolted from the table with a cookie in his hand. "Daddy, look at the cookie I colored."

"Looks great. Which one do I get?" Gavin asked.

Sam looked longingly at the cookie. "I'll go fix another one for you," he said and rushed back to the table.

Gavin met Sara's gaze. "Baking?"

"Very loosely," she said. "As you know, cooking isn't on my résumé, but Princess Bridget told me about the roll of cookie dough you can buy at the store. Genius," she said.

He wondered how she had never heard of the cookies before. What kind of life had prevented her both from cooking and knowing about rolls of cookie dough? Gavin hoped to get the answers to his questions about Sara soon.

"We would love for you to join us," she said with a mischievous smile on her face. "Maybe you could draw a frog on a cookie."

Just as he was about to refuse, Sam interrupted. "Yeah, Daddy. You should make a frog cookie."

Gavin lifted a dark eyebrow. "Okay," he said. "I'll give it a shot. Maybe all three of us should make frog cookies."

Sam gave a big nod of enthusiasm.

Chuckling to himself, Gavin washed his hands and sat down at the table. Sara had no idea of her impact on him and the family. He tried drawing a frog on two different cookies. Sara gave it a go and so did Sam.

Adelaide began to fuss, so Sara wiped the baby's hands and face and pulled her out of her chair. "Someone's ready for a nap. Sam, you'll need to take a rest this afternoon, too."

"But what about the cookies?" he asked.

"They'll be here when you wake up. Remember we're going to the palace tree lighting tonight, so both you and Adelaide will probably have a late bedtime."

"But what about my frog cookie?" he asked.

"I'll put it in a special place, so no one will eat it," she promised.

"I do think we should review our attempts at drawing a frog cookie," Gavin said.

She smiled at him. "Ah. A competitor at heart. Okay, here's mine," she said. "I think it looks more like a blob than a frog." Adelaide fussed and Sara gave her a jiggle as she studied Sam and Gavin's artwork. "Sam's is excellent. Look at the feet and the spots. Good job, Sam," she said, then looked at Gavin's frogs. "Nice job with the eyes. You used chocolate sprinkles. Very artistic. Sam must get his artistic talent from his dad. Do you want me to put yours in a special place, Gavin?"

"Absolutely not," Gavin said. "I plan to eat both of them."

"Daddy," Sam said, clearly shocked as he watched Gavin gobble both of the cookies. "I thought we were supposed to save them."

"I said you could have two," Sara said. "How many have you eaten?"

Sam gave a forlorn sigh. "Two," he said in a low voice.

"You can have one more later," Gavin said. "Come on. We'll read a book before you rest."

After he read two short books to Sam, Gavin closed his son's door behind him and glanced down the hallway. He noticed that the door to Sara's room was barely cracked open and as he walked closer, he heard the rustle of paper. He gently tapped on her door and pulled it open.

He saw toys and wrapping paper on the floor. "Do you ever take a break?"

"I really have to seize the moment with the wrapping. I can't do it when they're awake. The good news is I only have a few left to wrap."

"I can help," he said as he sank onto the floor across from her.

"Not necessary," she said.

"They're my kids. I insist," he said.

She blinked at the sharp tone in his voice and he frowned at himself in frustration. "Sorry," he said. "My wife rarely allowed me to do much with the kids. I think she just felt like she did it better."

"Hmm," Sara said and gave him some wrapping paper. "Perhaps she was a perfectionist," she said, shrugging. "No matter. The children will be more interested in the gifts than the wrapping paper. Well, Sam will. I can't say for sure what will interest Adelaide. Anything can be a toy when you're seven months old."

"Speaking of Christmas gifts, I asked you before, but you still haven't told me what you want for Christmas, Sara."

She glanced up at him, surprise widening her eyes. Then she looked down and sighed. "Just a few impossible things, most I can't name."

"To find your brother," he said.

She nodded. "I also wouldn't mind the opportunity to have twenty-four hours of sleep, all at one time. I already told you that," she said with a wicked smile. He suspected she was trying to keep the conversation light. "What about you? What would you like for Christmas?"

He paused a half beat. "Answers," he said.

She met his gaze and he saw turmoil in her eyes like the ocean during a storm. "I'm sorry. I can't do that, but someday soon I hope I can."

Gavin felt the door close in his face and his frustration ratcheted up another notch.

Hours later, Sara and Gavin fed the children and dressed them for the tree-lighting ceremony. Sara packed an extra diaper and bottle just in case the event went a little long for Adelaide. Gavin had been quiet since they'd finished gift-wrapping this afternoon. She knew he was frustrated. She knew he wanted more. Sara did, too, but she couldn't see any way around her oath of silence. At least, not in the immediate future.

Lately, when she'd awakened in the middle of the night, unable to go back to sleep, she'd fantasized about getting a fake passport and running away to try to find Alex, but she would have to leave Tabitha behind and completely alone. And as time wore on, she felt more protective of the children. How hard would it be for her to abruptly leave them?

Again, as she had done for the past year, she tried to push the disturbing thoughts from her mind and focus on what she could do this moment, and what she could do this moment was to help the Sinclair family experience a little joy and peace this Christmas.

Gavin drove to the palace where hundreds of cars already lined the sides of the streets. Sara and Gavin had been given a special parking pass so they would be able to park.

Gavin gave a low whistle. "Big turnout," he said.

"I get the impression that the Devereaux family is quite popular with the citizens of Chantaine, so there's bound to be a lot of excitement when there's a royal appearance open to the public. The family and the country are fortunate to enjoy their peace and financial stability," she said, thinking of the strife Sergenia suffered.

"You sound pretty passionate about that," he said. "It makes me wonder where you lived before you came to Chantaine."

Sara bit her lip. She should have kept her mouth shut or just found a different way to express herself. The problem was that as each day passed, she felt more like a leaking container, and little bits of her seeped out. "Many people are more aware of the wish for peace at Christmas. I'm no exception," she said as he pulled into a parking spot. "We'd better find a good spot, so the children can see."

In fact, when the palace guard saw their parking pass, he led them to an area reserved for special guests of the royal family. "What an honor," Sara said.

Palace staff offered LED candles to the guests with instructions to light them when Prince Stefan gave the sign. "I'm so glad these aren't real candles," she admitted to Gavin. "I think we've had enough fire in our lives lately. Don't you?"

Gavin shot her a sexy glance. "Depends on what kind of fire you're talking about."

Sara felt a rush of physical awareness at the expression on his face. When he gave her that certain look, it was too easy to think of how good it felt to be in his arms and to be pleasured by him. In her mind, she could hear his sexy groans of approval. Heat crept up to her face and she let out a little whoosh of air.

"Feeling warm?"

"Suddenly, yes," she admitted as she tried to get her hormones under control. "Oh, look," she said. "Here comes the royal family."

Murmurs of excitement rolled through the crowd and Sara could feel the affection the citizens had for the royal family. Prince Stefan stepped forward. "Greetings to the wonderful citizens of Chantaine." The crowd erupted in applause.

"Thank you for joining us for the lighting of the palace Christmas tree. This season we are especially aware of our wish for hope, love and peace for the entire world. We are grateful for the peace our country continues to experience, and we are humbled by the commitment of the citizens of Chantaine to pursue peace and service here and throughout the world. You serve as a beacon of light to the rest of the world."

The crowd applauded again with several people giving shouts of approval.

Stefan nodded. "And now, we'll bring out the rest of our growing family to join us."

Several palace nannies led the royal children to stand with their parents or, in the case of the babies, to be held in their arms. The crowd gave a collective "Aw." Sara couldn't blame them. The royal children were decked out in festive clothing and looked adorable.

"That's a lot of royal kids," Gavin said in a low voice. "That Devereaux clan has been busy."

Sara chuckled at his observation. "Such a happy sight."

"The royal family of Chantaine wishes you the happiest Christmas ever full of love, hope and peace." With that, the entire family, including the children, waved to the crowd. "If you have candles, light them as we light the tree," he said, giving a nod to the guard in charge of the lights.

The crowd erupted again, and Sara lit her candle and allowed Adelaide to hold it. Gavin helped Sam with his and the boy lifted his light high above his head. Sara was braced for Adelaide to try to put the plastic candle in her mouth, but the baby seemed entranced with the light it emanated.

A children's choir sang a Christmas carol. As the children's voices rang through the night, Sara's eyes filled with tears at the sweetness of the sound and the message. She blinked, but one tear escaped.

She felt Gavin slide his arm around her waist. "Are you okay?" he asked in a low voice.

She nodded. "It's just so peaceful and wonderful."

He nodded in agreement and brushed his lips over her forehead. Her heart was so full.

They stayed for the Christmas blessing given by a village priest and for the first song performed by the orchestra. Sam watched silently, then turned around and tugged on Gavin's shirt sleeve. "Look, Daddy," he said in an excited loud voice. "There's a man playing the piano just like Miss Sara does."

Sara felt her cheeks heat in self-consciousness.

"You're right," Gavin said and put his finger over his lips. "Indoor voice."

"But we're outside," Sam said.

At that point, Adelaide began to squirm and make fussy noises. "I think it may be time to go," she said and Gavin nodded in agreement.

They exited to the spot where Gavin had parked the car, and they loaded the children into their safety seats. As soon as they arrived home, Sara changed the baby's diaper, fed her a bottle and put her to bed while Gavin gave Sam a snack and put his son to bed.

She met Gavin in the hallway and he took her hand, leading her toward the den. "What a lovely evening," she said.

"Yeah. We got out just in time, considering Adelaide screamed most of the way home," he said, tugging her under the mistletoe. "You know what Sam would say right now, don't you?"

She smiled up at him. "Sam would say that since you're under the mistletoe, someone has to kiss you. And that someone is me." She lifted up on tiptoe to kiss him. Gavin put his arms around her and deepened the kiss. He pulled back after he'd left her breathless.

"Tonight was nice," he said. "Felt like family."

A crazy thrill raced through her at his words because she felt the same way. *It truly had felt as if they were a family.* She lifted her hand to touch his strong chin. A strong man with a strong but gentle soul, she thought. How had she gotten so lucky?

"I think I'm—" Her cell phone rang, interrupting her confession. She thought to ignore it, but so few people knew her number. Sighing, she gave a weak smile and pulled back. "Sorry. I should probably take this."

Glancing down at the phone, she saw that it was Tabitha. She immediately answered. "Hey, there. What's up?"

"I need you," Tabitha said with a sob.

Alarmed, Sara felt her heart take a dip. "Of course, I'll come to you. What is it? Are you ill?"

"Yes, but I hear it only lasts nine months. I'm pregnant," she wailed.

"Oh, dear. I'll be right there. Right away. I just need to tell Ga—" she corrected herself "—Mr. Sinclair. We will handle this."

She felt Gavin's curious gaze on her. "Who was that?"

A lump formed in her throat. *Another lie?* she taunted herself. She closed her eyes. "I'm not supposed to say. All I can tell you is that it is someone very dear to me and this is an emergency. I must go right now. I'll call the palace on the way and ask them to send a nanny in the morning. I'm sure they'll be more than willing to help."

Gavin took her hand. "You're as cold as ice. Are you sure there isn't some way I can help you? I don't want you driving when you're this upset."

"I'll be okay. It's just a shock," she said, trying to think of how she and Tabitha would handle this. The only thing she knew for sure was that they would get through it together.

"Of course, I'll let you go, but Sara," he said with a warning note in his voice, "I need answers, and I need them soon."

Chapter Thirteen

Sara coached herself to remain calm as she drove to Tabitha's apartment even though she didn't know how they were going to handle this. She scrambled for a plan. Princess Ericka would need to be told immediately. The Devereaux family would have to release them from the rule that Sara and Tabitha couldn't be seen together in public. If Sara was going to help Tabitha with the pregnancy and subsequently the child, then she couldn't continue to remain in hiding.

Perhaps the Devereaux clan would toss them out of Chantaine. Sara's heart raced in terror at the thought. That was the worst-case scenario. Right? No, there were worse things that could happen to her family. Some of those things had already happened.

Pulling in alongside Tabitha's apartment building, Sara took a deep breath and another then got out of her car and climbed the stairs to her sister's apartment. She barely knocked on the door before it was flung open and Tabitha pulled her inside.

Her sister's face was red from crying, and it broke Sara's heart to see her suffering. "Oh, sweetheart, come here." She held Tabitha in a close embrace. "It's going to be okay," she said as much for herself as for Tabitha. "It's going to be all right."

"How can it be okay?" Tabitha wailed, sobs racking her slim frame. "I'm pregnant. I'm going to have a baby, and I'm working in a restaurant under a fake name." Tabitha pulled back slightly. "Tell me, what about this is okay?"

Sara studied her sister's face. "I guess I should ask you if you want to keep the baby."

Tabitha stared at her in shock. "Of course, I'm keeping my baby."

"Well, that takes care of a few questions," Sara said. "Why don't we sit down?"

"I don't know if I can," Tabitha said. "I'm so terrified I feel like I'm going to shatter into a million pieces. What am I going to do?" she asked as she allowed Sara to guide her to the sofa.

"Sit down and I'll pour some tea for you. Do you have some chamomile?"

"Yes," Tabitha said, wringing her hands as she sank onto the sofa "This is such a mess. I've got to figure out how to make a living to support my child," Tabitha said, her voice jagged with panic.

Sara poured the tea and brought two cups into the den. She placed them on the table. "First, you've got to stop saying *I*. You are not in this alone. You and your child will have me by your side. I will help you provide for this child. We can and will work this out."

Tabitha picked up her cup and took a sip. "But what about our agreement with the Devereaux family? I don't know how we can hide the fact that we're sisters if you're helping me the way you say you plan to," she said. She pressed her lips together. "Thank you for being such a wonderful, dear sister to lousy me."

"Stop that. You're not lousy. I love you. I couldn't not be here for you," Sara insisted.

"That still doesn't solve our situation with the Devereaux family," Tabitha said.

"If they throw us out of the country, then we'll just find somewhere else to go. I don't think we can go back to Sergenia, but maybe tempers have cooled a little since we've left. It has been over a year."

"There was a lot of anger," Tabitha said.

"Yes, there was and we were the target. Now that the target has been removed, maybe people will realize that we actually didn't have much to do with the Sergenian economy, after all."

"That's very logical," Tabitha said. "But when people get into stressful situations, they're not always logical."

"We will work this out, Tabitha," Sara said, placing her hand over her sister's hand.

"How can you be so sure?"

"Look at what we've been through during the past year and a half," Sara said. "We've made it through despite all the threats, uncertainty and change. We can make it through this, too. So…about the father," she began, trying to tread lightly.

Tabitha took another sip of tea and took a shaky

breath. "It's Christoph. We used a condom every time except once. Who would have dreamed that when I was giving my cheeky advice to you, I was already pregnant?" she said in a dark tone. "He gave me his cell number, but he hasn't returned my calls."

"Are you in love with him? *Were* you in love with him?"

Tabitha grimaced. "I don't know. He was more of an escape for me. I could forget about how unhappy I was when I was with him. He made me laugh and he was very handsome. To be perfectly honest, I don't know if I could fall truly in love with anyone at the moment. As you know, our lives have been chaos central."

Sara nodded, although she was surprised by Tabitha's practical response about love. Sara couldn't be nearly so practical about her feelings for Gavin and the children.

"Well, I think you should take a hot shower and put on some clean nightclothes and let me tuck you in to bed," Sara said. "I'll sleep out here on the sofa. If you need me for anything, you can just call for me."

Tabitha's lower lip trembled. "How can you be so kind?"

"You would do the same thing for me," she said.

Tabitha took another deep breath. "Yes, I would."

"Okay, then get your shower. Things won't look so dire after you've gotten some rest. I'll call the restaurant tomorrow to tell them you're sick and you can't come in. You need a day to rest and let me pamper you with take-out food."

Tabitha reached toward her and hugged her tightly. "Thank you for coming."

After borrowing one of Tabitha's nightgowns, Sara

helped her sister into bed and then stretched out on the sofa. She stared up at the ceiling, wondering if she would get any sleep herself. For all the reassurance she'd given Tabitha, there was a lot to be figured out. Questions and possibilities whirled through her mind, making her more weary with each passing moment.

Sara told herself she couldn't solve all of this tonight, but they would make it work. Between the two of them, Sara knew that she and her sister had enough determination to conquer this newest challenge.

The next day, she burned the toast the first time she made it. The second time, it turned out fine. Tabitha awakened in a quiet mood. Sara hoped her sister would be able to find a bit of her sense of humor, but she understood it might take a while. Sara settled Tabitha on the sofa with a soft blanket and pillow where her sister watched mindless television and napped. During the afternoon while her sister rested, Sara made a trip to the market for soup, crackers and soda. Then she picked up some food from the bistro down the street.

By evening, Tabitha had sipped soup, eaten a sandwich and was ready to dig into the chicken Sara had brought her. "My appetite is so strange. One moment, I detest food. The next moment, I can't seem to get full."

"At least we know you don't have the flu or some horrid disease," Sara said.

"I've been thinking about it and this is going to turn my life upside down. But, as you said, our lives have already been turned upside down. Maybe this turn will make it all turn out right again."

Sara smiled as she watched her sister eat. "You sound much calmer today."

"Thank God you came over. I don't know how I could have survived that level of hysteria much longer."

That glimmer of humor gave Sara hope. Tabitha would find her way through this. "I'm going to stay another night," she began.

"No, you're not," Tabitha said. "That darling man and his darling children are probably lost without you. I'll be fine. I'm going back to work tomorrow."

"Are you sure?" Sara asked. "Maybe you should take another day."

"And do what? Sit on the sofa and feel sorry for myself?" Tabitha asked.

"The palace has provided a relief nanny for Gavin and the children," Sara continued. "It wouldn't hurt you to have another day of rest."

"Yes, it would. I'll just sit around and mope and worry. If I'm working, I'll be busy and solutions will come along when I'm not straining for them. So go," Tabitha said. "You came when I needed you, and I'm confident I'll be needing you again."

"If you're sure," Sara said, surprised at the quick return of Tabitha's independent nature.

"I'm sure," she said. "Now off you go."

"Only if you promise to call me if you need me for anything," Sara said.

"Yes, of course," Tabitha said.

"And you'll stay in touch and return your calls," Sara said.

"Now you're being a bit of a nag. I'm pregnant. Women have been doing this forever. There's no reason I can't muddle through it, too," she said. Then she smiled and stood and held out her arms. "One more hug, please."

Her heart filled with love and protectiveness, Sara gave her sister a big hug, then returned to the Sinclair house. She was eager to see Gavin and the children, but she dreaded the prospect of not answering Gavin's questions. She totally understood his need to know. If the tables were turned, she wasn't sure she would be able to be quite so patient.

Pulling into the driveway, she said a little prayer that her return would be smooth. She walked in the front door to find him sitting in the den working on his laptop. He looked up to see her. "You're back." He put his laptop aside and stood.

Her heart turned over at the sight of him. Just the sound of his voice made her feel so much better. She walked toward him. "Yes, I'm back. Are the children in bed?"

"Yes. They missed one of their naps during the day today, so they went down early. Is your emergency taken care of? Is everything okay?"

She smiled, although it took some effort. "I can say there's no more hysteria, and that's a good thing."

"Hysteria," he repeated. "Sounds mysterious."

"I wish I could tell you," she said.

"I'm not asking. Right now, anyway. But we do need to talk," he said. "Glass of wine?"

She shook her head. Something about his tone was serious and unwavering. She felt a strange sense of foreboding and told herself to stop. If he wasn't going to ask questions about all her secrets, then it couldn't be so bad. Right?

"Let's sit down," he said, leading her to the sofa.

Again, she felt that niggle of nerves, but pushed it aside. She sat a little bit away from him and waited.

"I've received some good news. We've caught up on the project and it will be finished ahead of schedule," he said.

"That's fantastic news. Congratulations," she said.

"Thank you. It wouldn't have been possible without your support of me and the children."

"Oh, I'm sure you would have managed it. You're the kind of man who gets things done."

He nodded. "I need to be making plans for my next position. I'm leaning toward taking the kids back to the States," he said.

Sara's stomach felt as if it had thudded to the floor. "Oh, that's right," she said. "Well, I'm sure you'll make the best decision for all of you."

"I want you to come with us," he said.

Surprise rendered her speechless. "Pardon me?"

"I want you to come with us. The children have flourished under your care. I'll pay you very well and make sure you take your vacation days. You don't seem to have anything holding you here in Chantaine. After all, you just arrived last year, so I can't believe you've put down roots."

Sara blinked. His offer was both exhilarating and heartbreaking. He was determined to keep her with his family, but he knew offering her anything more than a job would have been crazy. She was devastated by the idea of not having Gavin and the children in her life. She'd known she'd grown attached to them, but the reality of them leaving wrenched at her.

Her insides felt as if she were being torn apart. "I don't know what to say."

"Say yes," he said.

Sara closed her eyes. Her inner turmoil was so strong, she felt nauseated. "I can't," she finally managed.

"Why?" he asked.

She inhaled a sharp, painful breath. "I can't tell you."

Gavin's face hardened. "Is it to do you with all your secrets? Something about your emergency?"

"Yes," she whispered. "It is."

"Sara, this is important. I thought you loved my children," he said.

"I do," she said. "I do. Much more than I thought possible."

"I can't imagine anything that would keep you from sticking with us, then. You're not married, are you?"

"Oh, no," she said. "No."

"Are you a criminal?"

"Absolutely not," she said. "I just can't come with you. I can't."

"I wish I could believe you," he said. "But to turn this down with no explanation—" He broke off. "Maybe you care, but you just don't care enough. Don't worry," he said bitterly, rising from the couch. He picked up his laptop and looked down at her. "We'll just have to get by without you. You need to at least let the children know, so they won't grow more attached to you than they already have."

Sara watched him walk away and felt as if she'd been stabbed in an artery and left to die. The pain was so intense she doubled over from it. Taking deep breaths, she tried to tell herself to calm down. She was overreacting. She'd known her relationship with Gavin and his children wasn't forever. She'd known it. She'd reminded herself every day. This wasn't a surprise, she tried to tell herself.

Sara realized that she might have known it in her mind, but she hadn't known it in her heart. Feeling utterly broken, she forced herself to rise from the sofa and go to her room. She went through the motions of brushing her teeth and washing her face, then went to bed. Her heart hurt so much that she couldn't imagine going to sleep. Something inside her broke open like a river of pain. Suddenly, she began to cry. Deep gusts of tears burst from her. She tried not to sob because she didn't want anyone to hear her, but her grief over her missing brother and all the upheaval and, most difficult of all, losing Gavin and the children put her over the top.

She'd tried to hold it all together for so long, but now at this moment she just couldn't.

Sara wasn't sure when she'd fallen asleep but she awakened with a headache, salty cheeks and burning eyes. If this was love, she wasn't sure she was a good candidate for it. It was far too messy and was actually the worst thing she'd ever experienced. This was worse than being lost in a fire and suffering from burns and smoke inhalation as a child. Dragging herself from bed, she stood under the shower for a few minutes and waited to feel like a normal human being again. After her skin shriveled, she suspected normal wasn't in the cards for her today.

Pulling on her clothes, she put her hair in a loose bun and stiffened her spine as she walked toward the kitchen. By the sound of Gavin's and the children's voices, she could tell that the children were already awake and he was probably giving them breakfast. She stepped into the room. "Good morning," she said brightly.

"Mornin', Miss Sara," Sam said, his mouth full of cereal. "Can we make cookies again today?"

"I'm not sure there are any left, but we can if there are."

She glanced at Gavin and he gave her a quick nod before looking away from her as if he wished she didn't exist. Another stab, she thought, and she bit the inside of her cheek at the pain.

"Did you have fun with Binnie?"

Sam nodded. "She took us outside and made me run around the yard a lot."

"I'll bet she did," Sara said, smiling at Adelaide. "And how are you this morning, sweetness?" Adelaide paused in picking up one piece of cereal at a time to beam at her. "It must be a good day if you're not pulling at your ears or mouth.

"No teething at the moment?" she asked Gavin.

"No sign of it, but that could change. You'll excuse me, but I need to get to work. Binnie said for you to call her anytime if you need backup. I've arranged for her to cover this coming Saturday. I believe that's your scheduled day off," he said.

"I hadn't thought about it. I'm flexible," she said.

"No need. We've got this under control," he said as he left the kitchen.

He was so cold she wondered if she would get freezer burn. Her heart longed for his flirty smile and kind eyes. But she wasn't likely to see them ever again, she told herself.

Sara took enormous comfort from her time with the children. She knew she would have to tell them that she couldn't go with them when they left, but in the meantime, she cherished every moment in their presence. When Gavin arrived home, he gave her the same dismissive gaze he'd given her this morning. It pierced her soul, and that night she surprised herself by crying again.

Sara couldn't remember feeling this overwhelmed by her emotions. She did know, however, that she needed to talk to the Devereaux family about Tabitha's pregnancy. In the past, she'd always channeled her requests and questions through Princess Ericka. This time, she asked to speak to both Prince Stefan and Princess Ericka. There was too much at stake and the Devereaux family deserved to have this information in order to make plans.

Nervous, she paced outside Stefan's office. His assistant waved her in. "His Royal Highness and Her Highness will see you now," he said. Sara followed him inside the office. Stefan stood with Eve and two of his children. A gorgeous little girl with curly hair and blue eyes was coloring in a coloring book. The little boy was running his car around the edge of the carpet. Eve and Ericka chatted while Stefan talked on the phone.

Eve glanced up. "Well, come on in," Eve said, and Sara felt the woman study her face. "Are you feeling okay? You look a little blue under the eyes, like you're not getting enough sleep. I know that same feeling and look. That's why I ask," she said.

"I'm fine. Just busy with the recent move and Christmas coming up so soon."

"I understand," she said. "I love Christmas, but I'm looking forward to January, too."

"It's good to see you. I hope the house is working well," Ericka said.

"The house is lovely," Sara said.

Stefan finished his call and stood. "Miss Tarisse," he said, extending his hand. "How can we help you?"

"Your Highness," she said to Stefan.

He gave a crooked grin. "And you. Please have a seat."

"Oh, do you need me to take the children out?" Eve asked. "After your meeting with Stefan, we're dragging him away from his office for a little family outing.

"The subject matter is a little sensitive, but I suspect it will go right over their heads," she said as she sat down.

Eve's eyes widened and she glanced at her children. "They look pretty busy to me, so I think it should be fine."

"Thank you for agreeing to see me. I'll try to keep this short. When my sister and I were invited to take refuge in Chantaine, we were told that for the sake of safety, we needed to change our identities."

Stefan and Ericka nodded. "I know it's been difficult at times."

"It has," Sara said. "But what's been more difficult is that my sister and I were not supposed to be seen together in public. With our brother still missing and our lives turned upside down, we really would have benefited from being able to live with each other and support each other."

Ericka gave a glance of sympathy. "Chantaine is an international destination. We were just so concerned about the threats, and we were afraid you would be more likely to be recognized if you were together."

"The reason I'm here is because we're not going to be able to avoid being seen together in public any longer, and I just think it's fair that I tell you before we make that change," Sara said.

Stefan tilted his head and she could see that he'd earned his reputation for intimidation just by his expression. "And why is that?"

"Because my sister is pregnant and she is going to need my help," Sara said.

With the exception of Stefan's son making car sounds, the room turned utterly silent.

"Well, I guess that makes it a different kettle of fish," Eve said with her Texan twang.

"This wasn't planned," Sara said. "We understand if you want us to leave Chantaine."

"Oh, that's ridiculous," Eve said.

"Absolutely not," Ericka added.

All eyes turned to Stefan. He cleared his throat. "Perhaps we can work something out."

"I don't understand why this has to be such a big secret," Eve said. "They've been gone for a year. They're clearly not bleeding any money from their country. Did you take any expensive souvenirs when you left?" Eve asked.

"Oh, no. A couple of suitcases, but we left everything, including the family jewels, behind," Sara said.

"I think it's time to let our international security representative and your contacts in Sergenia know that the sisters are living here like church mice, so the citizens of Sergenia can stop blaming them for all their economic issues," Eve said.

Ericka pressed her lips together, appearing to cover her smile.

Stefan rubbed his hand over his face. "It may not be that easy. There are channels."

"And nobody wants to get on your bad side," Eve said.

"That's true," Ericka murmured as if she'd experienced Stefan's bad side.

Stefan sighed. "Okay. Let me see what I can do. I'll make some calls and try to get some answers in the next few days. In the meantime, how is your sister doing?"

"She was very upset and frightened when she first learned that she was pregnant, but she has calmed down. She has a bit of nausea, but she's managing it."

"Do stay on top of her condition. If she needs to be seen by the palace doctor, he's available to her."

And Sara liked him for that.

"And about the father?" he asked.

"I don't think he's going to be involved. He's not returning calls."

His jaw hardened in disapproval. "I'll get on this after my outing with the children. If she needs anything, please assure her that she is not alone. The resources of the palace are available to both of you."

"Thank you," she said. "I must ask one more favor. Is there any word of my brother, Alex? If we just knew if he was alive..."

"Our investigations have hit several walls regarding your brother. If it helps any, we have reason to hope he is alive. I'll try to get more information,"

Sara rose and left the room with Ericka by her side. Her eyes filled with tears and she furiously blinked them away.

Ericka looked at her. "Are you okay?"

Overwhelmed with gratitude, she swallowed over the lump in her throat. "I didn't know what to expect when I went into see the two of you. I'd braced myself for the possibility that you would want my sister and me to leave and that we would immediately need to begin searching for a safe haven."

Ericka put her arm around her. "Oh, Sara. We're not that heartless."

"I know *you* aren't, but Stefan has a lot on his shoulders. His decisions can affect a lot of people. Not just two princesses who fell out of favor in their home country."

"Don't spread it around, but my brother has the heart of a lion and a lamb. He's very protective and, even though he's a bit bossy at times, he's a wonderful man. Even more wonderful with Eve in his life. He'll work this out. He's an excellent negotiator. Try to enjoy the holiday. You've had enough on your shoulders."

"Thank you," Sara said. She was so relieved for Tabitha's sake, but this didn't change the fact that she had already lost Gavin and she would soon be saying goodbye to the children.

Sara stopped by a beach before she returned to the house. It was a little chilly, but the sight and sound of the waves coming in to shore soothed her. Surprising that she had grown up in a landlocked country, yet she connected so much with the ocean. She drew in the scent of the sea, willing it to heal all her hurts. After a little while, she returned to the house.

Gavin greeted her with questions in his gaze. "Another emergency?"

She shook her head. "It turned out better than I expected. I hope to be able to share it with you sometime. You mentioned that you wanted me to tell the children that I won't be able to go back to the States with you. Is it okay with you if I wait until after Christmas?"

"Yes," he said. "But don't wait too long."

Sara's heart broke again. She wondered how that was possible when she'd thought it was already shattered.

Chapter Fourteen

Christmas Eve arrived and Sara received a phone call from Ericka after lunch.

"I have good news for you," she said.

Nearly in tears with the report, Sara immediately called her sister to share the news. Tabitha also cried and promised to attend the gathering at Bridget's house that evening. Bridget had decided to host a Christmas Eve party in addition to Christmas dinner. Sara disconnected the call and knew what she had to do next. She needed to talk to Gavin. He had been so cold and disinterested during the past few days, and it was going to be difficult.

Mentally girding herself, she walked into the den and found Gavin playing a video game with Sam while Adelaide wormed her way across the carpet. Adelaide was days if not minutes away from crawling. Life would certainly be changing then, Sara thought. She wondered if Adelaide would crawl before Gavin and the children left for the States. She felt the stab of loss and wondered when the feelings of grief would end.

Sam glanced up from the video game. "Merry Almost Christmas, Miss Sara," he said.

Her heart turned over at the sweet greeting. "Merry Almost Christmas to you, Sam," she said in return. She then looked at Gavin without quite meeting his gaze. She couldn't bear to see the cool distance she'd found there during the past few days. "It's probably not the best time, but when you get a chance, I can give you a few answers to those questions you've been asking. And not asking," she added with a brittle laugh. "I'll give Adelaide her bottle and put her down." She scooped up the baby and took her back to the nursery.

As she rocked Adelaide, she whispered everything she wanted the baby to know for the rest of her life. "You're an amazing person. Already," Sara said. "And you're gorgeous. You will always be gorgeous, but it's more important to be gorgeous inside. You're going to be a strong, wonderful woman. I'm already proud of you," she whispered.

Smiling beneath the nipple of her bottle, Adelaide lifted her plump baby hand and brushed Sara's nose as if to say *You're a funny lady, but I like you.*

Sara chuckled softly. "I love you," she whispered. "I love you."

Adelaide finished the bottle and Sara lifted her to her shoulder. That was all it took to release any excess air. Then Sara put the baby in her bed and tried to memorize her features—her ivory skin and nearly invisible eyebrows, her plump rosy lips and shocking red hair. Such a precious sight.

Sighing, she turned around to find Gavin watching her from the doorway. She walked toward him and he closed the door behind her. "Sam's down for a nap."

"That was fast," she said.

"I'm curious," he said, his gaze still remote.

Oh, this was going to be difficult. She swallowed over the lump in her throat. She told herself he deserved to know the truth and even though it was too late for their relationship, she wanted to be fair.

They sat on the couch and she fought a sudden attack of nerves.

She saw a flash of concern in his eyes. "Are you sure you're okay? Do you want a glass of wine?"

She took a quick breath. "It's not my habit, but I think I'll have a sip, thank you. It's Christmas Eve," she said. *It's my moment of truth*, she thought.

Gavin returned with a glass of rosé.

"Thank you," she said. "Where do I start?" Her mind blurred. "Oh. I'm not sure how cohesive this is going to be, but I'll do my best. First, in answer to your question as to why I can't go to the States with you… There's no gentle way to say this—my sister is unexpectedly pregnant and she lives here."

"Your sister lives here?" he asked, confused.

"We were actually sent here. More on that in a moment. As I told you, this may not be completely cohesive. The father of my sister's baby is nowhere in sight. It appears he's not interested in being involved.

Gavin's face hardened. "She should find the father."

"She doesn't really want the father if he doesn't want her," Sara said. "And she's pretty sure she wasn't in love with him. She was careful, but things happen. She wants to keep the baby. I have to help her. My parents are dead. My brother is missing. I am all she has, so I must be here for her."

"That was the emergency," he concluded.

Sara nodded. "She was hysterical. We've had a tough couple of years. I had to assure her that she wasn't alone and that we would work this out."

"Then why can't we bring her with us?"

Sara's brain jammed. "Pardon me?"

"Why can't your sister come with us?"

Sara was so overcome with his immediate response that she began to cry. She shook her head, unable to speak. This kind of generosity was the last thing she had expected.

Gavin reached toward her. "What did I say? What did I do wrong?"

"Nothing," she said. "That offer was just so generous and loving and everything good. I'm overwhelmed."

"When you say you've had a bad couple of years, what do you mean?" he asked.

She sniffed. "I'm from a very small country called Sergenia. It's so small, you might not have even heard of it. Our country's economy slid into a terrible decline. We were blamed, banished and our lives threatened. That was why we came to Chantaine. The Devereaux family has been so wonderful to us," she said, knowing her words were spilling out in a disorganized form.

He shook his head. "Why were you banished? Did you do something to kill the economy?" He waved his hand in a sharp dismissive slice. "You know what, I don't care what your secrets are. I know who you really are and I'm in love with you. I want to marry you."

Sara was so shocked she almost passed out. She stared at him. "Can you please repeat that?"

"I love you," he said. "I've never met a person who made me feel more whole and challenged me at the same time. I want you in my life forever. Marry me, Sara," he said.

"Are you sure?" she whispered.

"I've known for a while now. I just hoped you felt the same way."

"Oh, I do," she said, flinging herself into his arms. "I didn't want to love you, but I did. And the children. I felt as if I would die without you, but I had promised I wouldn't reveal my past. There's more to tell," she added.

"The most important thing you can tell me is that you'll marry me. It doesn't have to be today or tomorrow, but let's make it soon."

"Yes," she said, feeling as if she'd been brought back to life. "I'll marry you." She trembled as she said the words, but in a good way, because she knew it was so right.

"I love you and I promise I'll do my best to make you happy," he said.

"You already have," she said. He took her in his arms and pressed his mouth against hers in a kiss of undying commitment.

Sara clung to him until she could hardly breathe. "I have more exciting news," she managed.

"What?"

"We have learned that my brother, Alexander, is alive. He sent a message through a complicated channel to reassure my sister and me. He's trying to do something for Sergenia, and he doesn't want anyone to know his whereabouts. I wish we could see him, but I can't tell you how relieved I am to know that he's alive and well. Another Christmas gift."

Gavin squeezed her. "I hate that you've suffered all of this by yourself. Promise me you won't keep secrets from me again. I swear I will always do whatever I can to help you."

"I will," Sasha said, her heart expanding at the depth of his commitment to her. She never dreamed a man like Gavin would love her with all his heart.

"There is one more thing," she said.

"I'm listening," he said.

"My real name is Sasha and I'm part of the royal family of Sergenia," she said.

Gavin pulled back and stared at her in disbelief. "Royal family?"

"It's why I can't cook," she said. "I'm a princess. A very broke princess."

"Does this mean I need to address you differently?"

"Yes, of course," she said with a mocking smile. "Your Highness is appropriate. Especially when I'm changing one of Adelaide's messy diapers."

He chuckled. "Your Highness. With you and Adelaide, I will have two princesses," he said. "Oh, including your sister, it will be three. How will I manage it?"

"I will help," she promised. She kissed him and she was too happy for words.

One month later, Sasha, wearing a wedding dress, stood across from Gavin in front of the village priest as they recited their wedding vows. She clung to his hands, feeling the presence of his children, her sister and the royal family witnessing their wedding.

She repeated her vows and he repeated his. They'd

added one personal promise they'd wanted to share during the ceremony.

"I will love you, cherish you and remind you how wonderful you are for the rest of my life," Sasha promised.

Gavin made the same vow.

"You may now kiss the bride," the priest announced. Gavin swept her into his arms and claimed her with a kiss. She held him tight and kissed him back.

"I can't believe I found you," he whispered.

"I'm so glad you did," she said, her heart so full of joy she could hardly stand it.

"I now present to you Mr. Gavin Sinclair and Mrs. Sasha Sinclair. May God bless this union and family."

Sasha and Gavin turned to the crowd. Gavin still held her hand securely in his. The witnesses alternately applauded and wiped away tears. Sam rushed both of them. "You said there was gonna be cake," he said. "When do we get the cake?"

Sasha and Gavin laughed. "Soon. Hang in there, buddy."

Just two weeks later, Sam awakened in the middle of the night. He didn't remember what he'd been dreaming, but he felt afraid. Very afraid. Usually when he woke up, he just listened to his ocean sound machine and he felt better. But tonight he still didn't feel good after listening to the sound machine.

Mama Sasha had told him that if he was ever afraid, he could come to her and Daddy in the middle of the night. Sliding out of bed, he pushed the door of his Daddy's bedroom open.

Daddy was snoring again, but his arm was around

Mama Sasha, and she was sleeping. Cookie, the new puppy, sat on the floor at the foot of the bed and thumped his tail. Something inside Sam felt all better and he went back to bed. He lay down and pulled up his covers. Everything was okay. Maybe Mama Sasha would even let him wear his new frog suit to preschool tomorrow.

* * * * *

SPECIAL EXCERPT FROM

When oilman Blair Coleman and the much younger Niki Ashton fall for one another, can the two overcome tragedy to find forever in each other's arms?

Read on for a sneak preview of WYOMING RUGGED, the latest WYOMING MEN *tale from* New York Times *bestselling author Diana Palmer.*

SHE SIGHED. HE WAS very handsome. She loved the way his eyes crinkled when he smiled. She loved the strong, chiseled lines of his wide mouth, the high cheekbones, the thick black wavy hair around his leonine face. His chest was a work of art in itself. She had to force herself not to look at it too much. It was broad and muscular, under a thick mat of curling black hair that ran down to the waistband of his silk pajamas. Apparently, he didn't like jackets, because he never wore one with the bottoms. His arms were muscular, without being overly so. He would have delighted an artist.

"What are you thinking so hard about?" he wondered aloud.

"That an artist would love painting you," she blurted out, and then flushed then cleared her throat. "Sorry. I wasn't thinking."

He lifted both eyebrows. "Miss Ashton," he scoffed, "you aren't by any chance flirting with me, are you?"

"Mr. Coleman, the thought never crossed my mind!"

"Don't obsess over me," he said firmly, but his eyes were still twinkling. "I'm a married man."

She sighed. "Yes, thank goodness."

His eyebrows lifted in a silent question.

"Well, if you weren't married, I'd probably disgrace myself. Imagine, trying to ravish a sick man in bed because I'm obsessing over the way he looks without a shirt!"

He burst out laughing. "Go away, you bad girl."

Her own eyes twinkled. "I'll banish myself to the kitchen and make lovely things for you to eat."

"I'll look forward to that."

She smiled and left him.

He looked after her with conflicting emotions. He had a wife. Sadly, one who was a disappointment in almost every way; a cold woman who took and took without a thought of giving anything back. He'd married her thinking she was the image of his mother. Elise had seemed very different while they were dating. But the minute the ring was on her finger, she was off on her travels, spending more and more of his money, linking up with old friends whom she paid to travel with her. She was never home. In fact, she made a point of avoiding her husband as much as possible.

This really was the last straw, though, ignoring him when he was ill. It had cut him to the quick to have Todd and Niki see the emptiness of their relationship. He wasn't that sick. It was the principle of the thing. Well, he had some thinking to do when he left the Ashtons, didn't he?

CHRISTMAS DAY WAS BOISTEROUS. Niki and Edna and three other women took turns putting food on the table for an unending succession of people who worked for the Ashtons. Most were cowboys, but several were executives from Todd's oil corporation.

Niki liked them all, but she was especially fond of their children. She dreamed of having a child of her own one day. She spent hours in department stores, ogling the baby things.

She got down on the carpet with the children around the Christmas tree, oohing and aahing over the presents as they opened them. One little girl who was six years old got a Barbie doll with a holiday theme. The child cried when she opened the gaily wrapped package.

"Lisa, what's wrong, baby?" Niki cooed, drawing her into her lap.

"Daddy never buys me dolls, and I love dolls so much, Niki," she whispered. "Thank you!" She kissed Niki and held on tight.

"You should tell him that you like dolls, sweetheart," Niki said, hugging her close.

"I did. He bought me a big yellow truck."

"A what?"

"A truck, Niki," the child said with a very grown-up sigh. "He wanted a little boy. He said so."

Niki looked as indignant as she felt. But she forced herself to smile at the child. "I think little girls are very sweet," she said softly, brushing back the pretty dark hair.

"So do I," Blair said, kneeling down beside them. He smiled at the child, too. "I wish I had a little girl."

"You do? Honest?" Lisa asked, wide-eyed.

"Honest."

She got up from Niki's lap and hugged the big man. "You're nice."

He hugged her back. It surprised him, how much he wanted a child. He drew back, the smile still on his face. "So are you, precious."

"I'm going to show Mama my doll," she said. "Thanks, Niki!"

"You're very welcome."

The little girl ran into the dining room, where the adults were finishing dessert.

"Poor thing," Niki said under her breath. "Even if he thinks it, he shouldn't have told her."

"She's a nice child," he said, getting to his feet. He looked down at Niki. "You're a nice child, yourself."

She made a face at him. "Thanks. I think."

His dark eyes held an expression she'd never seen before. They fell to her waistline and jerked back up. He turned away. "Any more coffee going? I'm sure mine's cold."

"Edna will have made a new pot by now," she said. His attitude disconcerted her. Why had he looked at her that way? Her eyes followed him as he strode back into the dining room, towering over most of the other men. The little girl smiled up at him, and he ruffled her hair.

He wanted children. She could see it. But apparently his wife didn't. What a waste, she thought. What a wife he had. She felt sorry for him. He'd said when he was engaged that he was crazy about Elise. Why didn't she care enough to come when he was ill?

"It's not my business," she told herself firmly.

It wasn't. But she felt very sorry for him just the same. If he'd married *her*, they'd have a houseful of children. She'd take care of him and love him and nurse him when he was sick...she pulled herself up short. He was a married man. She shouldn't be thinking such things.

SHE'D BOUGHT PRESENTS online for her father and Edna and Blair. She was careful to get Blair something impersonal. She didn't want his wife to think she was chasing him or anything. She picked out a tie tac, a *fleur de lis* made of solid gold. She couldn't understand why she'd chosen such a thing. He had Greek ancestry, as far as she knew, not French. It had been an impulse.

Her father had gone to answer the phone, a call from a business associate who wanted to wish him happy holidays, leaving Blair and Niki alone in the living room by the tree. She felt like an idiot for making the purchase.

Now Blair was opening the gift, and she ground her teeth together when he took the lid off the box and stared at it with wide, stunned eyes.

"I'm sorry," she began self-consciously. "The sales slip is in there," she added. "You can exchange it if..."

He looked at her. His expression stopped her tirade midsentence. "My mother was French," he said quietly. "How did you know?"

She faltered. She couldn't manage words. "I didn't. It was an impulse."

His big fingers smoothed over the tie tac. "In fact, I had one just like it that she bought me when I graduated from college." He swallowed. Hard. "Thanks."

"You're very welcome."

His dark eyes pinned hers. "Open yours now."

She fumbled with the small box he'd had hidden in his suitcase until this morning. She tore off the ribbons and opened it. Inside was the most beautiful brooch she'd ever seen. It was a golden orchid on an ivory background. The orchid was purple with a yellow center, made of delicate amethyst and topaz and gold.

She looked at him with wide, soft eyes. "It's so beautiful..."

He smiled with real affection. "It reminded me of you, when I saw it in the jewelry store," he lied, because he'd had it commissioned by a noted jewelry craftsman, just for her. "Little hothouse orchid," he teased.

She flushed. She took the delicate brooch out of its box and pinned it to the bodice of her black velvet dress. "I've never had anything so lovely," she faltered. "Thank you."

He stood up and drew her close to him. "Thank you, Niki." He bent and started to brush her mouth with his, but forced himself to deflect the kiss to her soft cheek. "Merry Christmas."

She felt the embrace to the nails of her toes. He smelled of expensive cologne and soap, and the feel of that powerful body so close to hers made her vibrate inside. She was flustered by the contact, and uneasy because he was married.

She laughed, moving away. "I'll wear it to church every Sunday," she promised without really looking at him.

He cleared his throat. The contact had affected him, too. "I'll wear mine to board meetings, for a lucky charm," he teased gently. "To ward off hostile takeovers."

"I promise it will do the job," she replied, and grinned.

Her father came back to the living room, and the sudden, tense silence was broken. Conversation turned to politics and the weather, and Niki joined in with forced cheerfulness.

But she couldn't stop touching the orchid brooch she'd pinned to her dress.

TIME PASSED. Blair's visits to the ranch had slowed until they were almost nonexistent. Her father said Blair was trying to make his marriage work. Niki thought, privately, that it would take a miracle to turn fun-loving Elise into a housewife. But she forced herself not to dwell on it. Blair was married. Period. She did try to go out more with her friends, but never on a blind date again. The experience with Harvey had affected her more than she'd realized.

Graduation day came all too soon. Niki had enjoyed college. The daily commute was a grind, especially in the harsh winter, but thanks to Tex, who could drive in snow and ice, it was never a problem. Her grade point average was good enough for a magna cum laude award. And she'd already purchased her class ring months before.

"Is Blair coming with Elise, do you think?" Niki asked her father as they parted inside the auditorium just before the graduation ceremony.

He looked uncomfortable. "I don't think so," he said. "They've had some sort of blowup," he added. "Blair's butler, Jameson, called me last night. He said Blair locked himself in his study and won't come out."

"Oh, dear," Niki said, worried. "Can't he find a key and get in?"

"I'll suggest that," he promised. He forced a smile. "Go graduate. You've worked hard for this."

She smiled. "Yes, I have. Now all I have to do is decide if I want to go on to graduate school or get a job."

"A job?" he scoffed. "As if you'll ever need to work."

"You're rich," she pointed out. "I'm not."

"You're rich, too," he argued. He bent and kissed her cheek, a little uncomfortably. He wasn't a demonstrative man. "I'm so proud of you, honey."

"Thanks, Daddy!"

"Don't forget to turn the tassel to the other side when the president hands you your diploma."

"I won't forget."

THE CEREMONY WAS LONG, and the speaker was tedious. By the time he finished, the audience was restless, and Niki just wanted it over with.

She was third in line to get her diploma. She thanked the dean, whipped her tassel to the other side as she walked offstage and grinned to herself, imagining her father's pleased expression.

It took a long time for all the graduates to get through the line, but at last it was over, and Niki was outside with her father, congratulating classmates and working her way to the parking lot.

She noted that, when they were inside the car, her father was frowning.

"I turned my tassel," she reminded him.

He sighed. "Sorry, honey. I was thinking about Blair."

Her heart jumped. "Did you call Jameson?"

"Yes. He finally admitted that Blair hasn't been sober for three days. Apparently, the divorce is final, and Blair found out some unsavory things about his wife."

"Oh, dear." She tried not to feel pleasure that Blair

was free. He'd said often enough that he thought of Niki as a child. "What sort of things?"

"I can't tell you, honey. It's very private stuff."

She drew in a long breath. "We should go get him and bring him to the ranch," she said firmly. "He shouldn't be on his own in that sort of mood."

He smiled softly. "You know, I was just thinking the same thing. Call Dave and have them get the Learjet over here. You can come with me if you like."

"Thanks."

He shrugged. "I might need the help," he mused. "Blair gets a little dangerous when he drinks, but he'd never hit a woman," he added.

She nodded. "Okay."

BLAIR DIDN'T RESPOND to her father's voice asking him to open the door. Muffled curses came through the wood, along with sounds of a big body bumping furniture.

"Let me try," Niki said softly. She rapped on the door. "Blair?" she called.

There was silence, followed by the sound of footsteps coming closer. "Niki?" came a deep, slurred voice.

"Yes, it's me."

He unlocked the door and opened it. He looked terrible. His face was flushed from too much alcohol. His black, wavy hair was ruffled. His blue shirt, unbuttoned and untucked, looking as if he'd slept in it. So did his black pants. He was a little unsteady on his feet. His eyes roved over Niki's face with warm affection.

She reached out and caught his big hand in both of hers. "You're coming home with us," she said gently. "Come on, now."

"Okay," he said, without a single protest.

Jameson, standing to one side, out of sight, sighed with relief. He grinned at her father.

Blair drew in a long breath. "I'm pretty drunk."

"That's okay," Niki said, still holding tight to his hand. "We won't let you drive."

He burst out laughing. "Damned little brat," he muttered.

She grinned at him.

"You dressed up to come visit me?" he asked, looking from her to her father.

"It was my graduation today," Niki said.

Blair grimaced. "Damn! I meant to come. I really did. I even got you a present." He patted his pockets. "Oh, hell, it's in my desk. Just a minute."

He managed to stagger over to the desk without falling. He dredged out a small wrapped gift. "But you can't open it until I'm sober," he said, putting it in her hands.

"Oh. Well, okay," she said. She cocked her head. "Are you planning to have to run me down when I open it, then?"

His eyes twinkled. "Who knows?"

"We'd better go before he changes his mind," her father said blithely.

"I won't," Blair promised. "There's too damned much available liquor here. You only keep cognac and Scotch whiskey," he reminded his friend.

"I've had Edna hide the bottles, though," her father assured him.

"I've had enough anyway."

"Yes, you have. Come on," Niki said, grabbing Blair's big hand in hers.

He followed her like a lamb, not even complaining at

her assertiveness. He didn't notice that Todd and Jameson were both smiling with pure amusement.

WHEN THEY GOT back to Catelow, and the Ashton ranch, Niki led Blair up to the guest room and set him down on the big bed.

"Sleep," she said, "is the best thing for you."

He drew in a ragged breath. "I haven't slept for days," he confessed. "I'm so tired, Niki."

She smoothed back his thick, cool black hair. "You'll get past this," she said with a wisdom far beyond her years. "It only needs time. It's fresh, like a raw wound. You have to heal until it stops hurting so much."

He was enjoying her soft hand in his hair. Too much. He let out a long sigh. "Some days I feel my age."

"You think you're old?" she chided. "We've got a cowhand, Mike, who just turned seventy. Know what he did yesterday? He learned to ride a bicycle."

His eyebrows arched. "Are you making a point?"

"Yes. Age is only in the mind."

He smiled sardonically. "My mind is old, too."

"I'm sorry you couldn't have had children," she lied and felt guilty that she was glad about it. "Sometimes they make a marriage work."

"Sometimes they end it," he retorted.

"Fifty-fifty chance."

"Elise would never have risked her figure to have a child," he said coldly. "She even said so." He grimaced. "We had a hell of a fight after the Christmas I spent here. It disgusted me that she'd go to some party with her friends and not even bother to call to see how I was. She actually said to me the money was nice. It was a pity I came with it."

"I'm so sorry," she said with genuine sympathy. "I can't imagine the sort of woman who'd marry a man for what he had. I couldn't do that, even if I was dirt-poor."

He looked up into soft, pretty gray eyes. "No," he agreed. "You're the sort who'd get down in the mud with your husband and do anything you had to do to help him. Rare, Niki. Like that hothouse orchid pin I gave you for Christmas."

She smiled. "I wear it all the time. It's so beautiful."

"Like you."

She made a face. "I'm not beautiful."

"What's inside you is," he replied, and he wasn't kidding.

She flushed a little. "Thanks."

He drew in a breath and shuddered. "Oh, God..." He shot out of the bed, heading toward the bathroom. He barely made it to the toilet in time. He lost his breakfast and about a fifth of bourbon.

When he finished, his stomach hurt. And there was Niki, with a wet washcloth. She bathed his face, helped him to the sink to wash out his mouth then helped him back to bed.

He couldn't help remembering his mother, his sweet French mother, who'd sacrificed so much for him, who'd cared for him, loved him. It hurt him to remember her. He'd thought Elise resembled her. But it was this young woman, this angel, who was like her.

"Thanks," he managed to croak out.

"You'll be all right," she said. "But just in case, I'm going downstairs right now to hide all the liquor."

There was a lilt in her voice. He lifted the wet cloth he'd put over his eyes and peered up through a growing massive headache. She was smiling. It was like the sun coming out.

"Better hide it good," he teased.

She grinned. "Can I get you anything before I leave?"

"No, honey. I'll be fine."

Honey. Her whole body rippled as he said the word. She tried to hide her reaction to it, but she didn't have the experience for such subterfuge. He saw it and worried. He couldn't afford to let her get too attached to him. He was too old for her. Nothing would change that.

She got up, moving toward the door.

"Niki," he called softly.

She turned.

"Thanks," he said huskily.

She only smiled, before she went out and closed the door behind her.